black girl talk

edited by the Black Girls

Sister Vision
Black Women and Women of Colour Press

ISBN 0-920813-03-8
1995 © Copyright Sister Vision Press
Individual selections © copyright by their respective author(s)

95 96 97 98 99 ML 0 9 8 7 6 5 4 3 2 1

This book is protected by the copyright laws of Canada and member countries of the Berne Convention. All rights are reserved. No part of this book may be reproduced or transmitted in any form or by any means without permission in writing from the publisher, except for reviews.

Canadian Cataloguing in Publication Data
Main entry under title:
Black Girl Talk

ISBN 0-9230813-03-8

1. Canadian literature (English) — Black-Canadian authors
2. Canadian literature (English) — Women authors
3. Youths' writings, Canadian (English)
4. Canadian literature (English) — 20th century
5. American literature — Afro-American authors
6. American literature — Women authors
7. Youths' writings, American
8. American literature — 20th century.

I. The Black Girls

PS8235.W6B53 1995   C810.8'092837   C95-932503-4
PR9194.5.W6B53 1995

Represented in Canada by the Literary Press Group
Distributed in Canada by General Distribution
Represented and distributed in the U.S.A. by InBook
Represented in Britain by Turnaround Distribution

Sister Vision Press acknowledges the financial support of the Canada Council and the Ontario Arts Council toward its publishing program.

Managing Editor: Makeda Silvera
Production: Stephanie Martin
Book Design & Typesetting: Michèle Lonsdale Smith
Photographs: cover, pgs 11, 28, 36, 148: David Zapparoli

Printed and bound in Canada by union labour

Published by:
SISTER VISION: Black Women and Women of Colour Press
P.O. Box 217, Station E
Toronto, Ontario, Canada M6H 4E2

*T*he **Black Girls** would like to thank
Makeda Silvera for the concept of this book,
and for her enthusiastic support and editorial guidance
during this project, and the three special sistahs who helped
to pull **BLACK GIRL TALK** together:
Maxine Greaves, Ayoola Silvera and Antoinette.
Thanks also to the girls on the cover: (from l to r)
Keisha Silvera, Makeda Lewis and Siobhan Douglas.
And to all the other sistahs who contributed — Thank you!

The Black Girls

Contents...

Introduction — Makeda Silvera ix

my sistahs

Chillin' With My Girls — Kim Outten 1
Sister Love — Marta Kateri Ferede 2
I Am — Tonia Bryan & Nicole Redman 139
To Christine — Susan Forde 145
Sister–Sister — Joi-Elle Dinnall 146

my history, my identity

"To Finish What Has Begun" —
    Maxine Greaves, Marta Kateri Ferede, Sistah Caroline 3
School Daze — Susan Forde 22
Educate — Shelley Rodney 22
Telling It Like It Is — Titilola Adebanjo, Jillian M. Dixon, Tovah Leiha Dixon,
    Marie-Jolie Rgwigema Didas Gemeni 23
With Out You — Stacey Tingle 49
Drum Beats — Asha Noel 64
Recipe For A Negro — Lisa Hollingsworth 97
Colour Me Bad: The Experience of A Dark-Skinned Woman —
    Ibiyomi Jegede 116
Subliminal Demise — Valery Mendes 142

my father

A Conversation With My Father — *Susan Forde* 14

my brothas

Brothas — *Jay Pitter* 81
Gangsta Bitch, Diva Hip Hop, Goddesses & Earth Women
    & Hip Hop Culture — *Maxine Greaves with Motion* 122
Why Sistahs Don't Like to Nike — *Sistah Caroline* 134

love & relationships

Untitled — *Wendy A. Vincent* 15
Sporting Womanhood — *Joi-Elle Dinnall* 34
When I Taste the Love — *Anna Bauer* 35
A Black Woman's Haiku — *Lisa Hollingsworth* 36
You Said You Loved Me And I Was Your Woman — *Roxanne Tracy* ... 87
My Ex — *Kim Outten* 96
Eulogy — *Antoinette* 114
Sweetness — *Frances Opoku* 118

my hair

And Look What The Future Has Wrought — *Mansa* 16
My Personal Beast — *Erica Lawson* 18

memories

First Ride — *Natalie Eta* 20
Memory-Bank Movies — *Suzanne Anderson* 68
Room 9K — *Ayoola Silvera* 72
Darling — *Antoinette* 144

sex and sexuality

Naked — *Karen Lee* 37
Dark Berry — *Charmaine Lewis* 39
Two Bodies–One Lover — *Lorraine Anne McLeod* 41
Interlude — *Nicole Minerve* 42
Pears Of Green & Yellow — *Camille Bailey* 43
York? Homos? Really? — *Maxine Greaves* 45
Going Without — *Suzanne Anderson* 47

racism

Hurt — *Tara Darrall* 52
Talking Back In Class — *Valery Mendes* 54
The Man Who Called Me Nigger — *Sherrie Outten* 63
Rainbow of Love — *Ellaree Metz* 98
Holding Out On Stereotypes — *Melissa Smith* 120

violence & abuse

Patriarchy — *Carol Higgins* 65
The Art of Possession–Strange Relationship — *Mansa* 66
Rewind My Selecta! — *Karen Lee* 82
United We Stand, Departed We Fall — *Ngardy Conteh* 86
Unrest — *Monique Wilson* 89
Untitled — *Yvette Trancoso* 90
The Body — *Jennifer Holland* 102
The Occurrence — *Paula Avril French* 103
We Are Family — *Valery Mendes* 110

addiction

Hit of Poison — *Ellaree Metz* 100
Uncontrollable Feeling — *Wendy Davis* 101

i stand up

Normal People — *Ayoola Silvera* 50
Dismissed — *Natasha Gomez-Bonner* 73
The Pussy Is Ours — *Ijose* 74
Brothas — *Jay Pitter* 81
Don't Touch It — *Yvette Trancoso* 92
When I was Real — *Mansa* 94
Uncontrollable — *Marta Kateri Ferede* 119
Here She Comes — *Sherrie Outten* 138

bios
.... 151

intro...

BLACK GIRL TALK is a project initiated by Sister Vision Press to bring the voices of young Black Women together in poetry, prose, essay, dialogue, art work and other forms of expression.

We offer this long-awaited collection as an affirmation of the talents of young Black Women, and to combat some of the negative stereotypes about youth. We know from experience that this is often a very frustrating period for young adults, fraught with insecurities, pain, confusion, excitement, joy and discovery.

BLACK GIRL TALK brings it all together — the voices are urgent and we recognize them immediately.

The stories and poetry speak of the confusion of young adulthood and are filled with bursts of energy, crazy love, and sisterly bonding.

They also bring to your face issues around death, racism, parental conflict, male dominance, substance abuse and sexual abuse.

The three dialogue/tape discussions offer a rare and honest glimpse into the lives of young Black Women. **To Finish What Has Begun** and **Telling It Like It Is** touch on issues relating to community, friends, family tensions, school, racism and gender inequalities.

In **Gangsta Bitch, Diva Hip Hop, Goddesses & Earth Women & Hip Hop Culture**, two women discuss political consciousness and politically incorrect lyrics. They talk about male rappers, and the negative stereotyping of women in Hip Hop culture. This piece is kicking.

In **York? Homos? Really?**, one of three essays, a 'Sistah' talks about being a womyn identified sistah—a Black Lesbian in her first year of university.

Talking Back In Class is a jarring piece on urban racism. Read it; there's not much more to say.

The Pussy Is Ours, another Black Woman pursuing the issue of heterosexual interracial relationships, is cutting; telling it like this Sister sees it. In this essay she passionately takes Black men and the patriarchal system to task.

BLACK GIRL TALK brings the 90's generation's urgent voices to print. These Sisters are proud, loud and bold. Listen to the talk.

In Sisterhood,

Makeda Silvera

Chillin' with my girls

It's my girls with whom I chill
but it's more than just that
when I can't hold my own
then they cover my back
it's like that
we have a special bond
that no one can touch
it's not my man I turn to
it's my girls that I can trust
been through the hard times
the rough times
the oh my god I'd rather die times
always know if I'm lying
when something's got me crying
or deep inside I'm dying
they know truly who I am
I love truly who they are
'cause if I really need someone
my girls are never far
we're like sisters
with a deep love for each other
we have a special bond
no disrespect to the brothers
we got a special thing
like nothin' in the world
ain't no man interferin'
when I'm chillin' with my girls

kim autten

sisteR LOVE

(for Roman)

marta kateri ferede

*r*elated by situation
But sisters by choice!
So proud, so grateful
To have you in my life.

Often I've wondered
Where I would be
If I hadn't had your strength
And love beside me.

I know at times our personalities clash
But no matter how many times they do,
Always remember Lil'sis that
I thank the day God brought you in my life.

denise johnson

"To Finish what has Begun"

HOST Welcome to the 'African Woman and Family' interview. We have with us in our studio three beautiful young women, strong African women, who are also writers. They will be contributing to a book called **Black Girl Talk**, published by SISTER VISION PRESS. I will be talking with them about their backgrounds, their experiences as young Black women, and the kind of contributions that they will be making to this important anthology.

host We have in the studio today **Sistah Caroline**, **Maxine Greaves** and **Marta Kateri Ferde**. I'm going to ask them to tell me a little bit about their background, because they have some interesting things to share with you. We'll start with Maxine.

maxine I was born in Toronto and I grew up mainly around the Jane and Finch area, but between the ages of 7 and 17, I spent a lot of time going back and forth between New York and Toronto. And, I have a four-year-old daughter.

host What's her name?

maxine Her name is Shelly. I recently finished high school, and graduated as Valedictorian. I'm currently a student at York University, and I've been writing for most of my life. You know, journals, when I was younger. And now I'm into songwriting, poetry, and short stories and one-act plays. I'm also the 1994 recipient of the Harry Jerome Award.

3

host Glad to have you on the show, my sister, and congratulations. Now we'll go to Marta Kateri Ferede. Please, my sister, can you share your history with us?

marta Sure. Let me tell you about realizations that came to me when I was young. I was four when I realized my existence in the world, six when I thought I was the most intelligent person in this whole universe, and about ten when, ah, I thought I was adopted by my Ethiopian parents (*laughter*). So you know I've had quite a bit of imagination ever since I was a young child. It also comes through my poetry. Poetry gives me a voice, to speak about things that have been silenced or that I have kept inside. I have lived in Toronto since I was seven; before that I lived in Ethiopia where I was born. I attend York University, where I major in Mass Communication and English. I hope that this book will unite Black sisters and African sisters, and that our voices will be heard. I think we have a lot of powerful things to say.

host Thank you my sister. You said you felt that you were an alien, that you were adopted by Ethiopians. Why? (*laughter*) What gave you that idea?

marta Well, I have a different sense of humour, a very different sense of just why I thought I was here. You know? I never seemed to fit. I was that little outsider of the family, you know? So I thought I was adopted. My parents thought that as well.(*laughter*)

host So you took to writing for it?

marta Yes. Yes.

host Next we will be talking to Sistah Caroline. Would you tell us a little bit about yourself? You describe yourself in an interesting way, as a womb-mon.

sistah caroline Yes, I am a woman; I am womb; I am nature; I am Black; I am poetry, Young Poets of the Revolution; I am theatre, Warriors for Revolutionary Suicide Sistahs; a dramatist; I am a writer, Original Poetry from the Voice of Feminine Power, plays like Black Curse. I have a B.A.A. in Radio and Television Arts from Ryerson Polytechnical University (Toronto, Canada), I've worked with the radio station, C.K.L.N. Woman and Hip Hop Show, we were never asked by Vision T.V., the Canadian Broadcasting Corporation, Morningside; I am community, I volunteer with Each-One-Teach-One, Fresh Arts, Toronto Black Achievers Program, Tropicana youth group, and the Rape Crisis Centre; I'm conscious; I'm X, I'm positive; I love myself.

marta You go girl! *(laughter)*

host Now, let's go into the reasons why you decided that you would contribute to this book. How was the name conceived?

maxine Well, the name **Black Girl Talk** comes out of a necessity for young Black women to say what they feel. I think it sort of symbolizes what we don't do enough of—talk.

host Okay, but some people argue that all we do as Black people is talk. Do you agree with that, or disagree?

sistah caroline I think we do talk a lot, but sometimes we don't really talk about issues. As young Black women, we can talk, but when we get together and start talking we never really get personal, we never get vulnerable and we never get honest. In my opinion, this is what this book is trying to encompass, that intimacy and that ability to say hey! there are other sisters out there that have had similar experiences so you don't have to feel like you're alone.

marta That's very interesting. I wanted to add something. There's a poem of mine, it deals with exactly that, how we seem to talk without saying anything, and one of the lines in it goes 'After the speech and sermon is done, no one wants to finish what has begun' and I think this book is a way of collecting all we're talking, and then doing something about it.

host Do you remember that piece?

marta Yes.

host Can you share it with us?

marta It's called "Revolution". And it goes:

I know some that talk of change
revolution
I know some that sing emancipation
revolution
I know some that scream for justice
revolution!
They wave their hands.
Be clapping and yelling and dancing too!
Revolution!
But after the speech and sermon is done
No one wants to finish what has begun.
If our ideas move our hands,
If our words inspire our hearts,
Then no one, no society can break us apart.
R e v o l u t i o n ! ! ! !

sistah caroline Good stuff.

marta Thank you.

host What motivated you to write this piece?

marta I think at that period of my life, I had just started university expecting a revolution. I wanted to go out there, join groups that were very politically involved. But then I found out that the main concern was who's having the best dance and what everybody was wearing. It just really threw me off. And I said we need to do something with the words that we say, instead of just leaving them in the air hanging and fading.

host Your parents died in a fire didn't they?

marta Yes, my parents passed away when I was 13 years old and so there's only my sister and I.

host What kind of experiences did you have in foster homes?

marta I was moved from foster home to foster home. There wasn't any Black foster homes, so I was moved into White homes. It was a very troubling time. I didn't know who I was, I lost that sense of meaning, that sense of identity.

host But has it made you stronger?

marta Yes. Sometimes when I think I'm at the weakest, I realize that things do not happen to us that we cannot handle.

host Yes, we can learn from even the worst things that happen in our lives. Sistah Caroline? I want to get back to the question of not talking, of being afraid to show our vulnerability. We're vulnerable sometimes but we don't want to take that to the streets so that it can be used against us. Have any of you come up with any methods or support systems to encourage other sisters who may be willing to speak, but don't know what the backlash will be when they write their life story or if they critique what they see happening around them?

maxine Well, for myself, a while back I formed a small support group within the community for young Black women, called the African Queens. They meet regularly and they talk about their personal experiences. They talk about their resentment about having to look after younger brothers and sisters and all that. They talk about boyfriends and all kinds of things. They are supporting each other without even organizing as a formal group.

sistah caroline Right…

host So, Caroline, did you want to make any comments regarding that?

sistah caroline Well, I do a lot of volunteer work concentrated around young Black people, especially Black women. I try to make myself accessible so that although, you know, I'm a performer, that doesn't mean I have a swelled head and you can't approach me and talk to me on a street level. I always try to remain visible and down to earth. I have mentors who are also in performance who didn't forget about me even though they are making albums, doing stage plays and so forth, so I try to follow the example that mentors like Lillian Allen, and Afua Cooper have set for me.

host I am particularly interested in the point Maxine raised, about young women having to look after young brothers and sisters. In our culture we support one another and Mom, 'cause normally it's Mom talking care of the babies and taking care of the children. When she has to go out to work, there's little support. What are some of the things that come out of that type of discussion with a group of young Black women?

sistah caroline Oh, you'd hear about all kinds of problems. Usually there are older brothers that get to go and do what they want and the girl child gets stuck with the children, and so she is angry. The women don't understand why, if they are old enough to look after the younger brothers and sisters, then why aren't the older brothers, who are even older than them, having to look after children?

In my family, there's my brother who is the youngest, and then there's 3 older sisters, so he was babied, and all the women cook and clean but not this little man 'cause he's 13 years old. My mother had to work several jobs because of economics and so forth.

host Sister Marta?

marta My mother is the strongest person that I have ever known in my life. In my country, where I was born, Ethiopia, women can't even own property. Women were in the kitchen. Men never went into the kitchen. Women had specific duties and if you went outside the boundaries you were looked upon as an outsider. And my mother said, 'I am going to get my education.' She put herself through school and she made a life for herself. She taught me that women don't have to be submissive. Women don't have to be quiet. Women can do anything that they want and I could do whatever I wanted to do and my dream was only as far and or high as I allowed it to be.

host How do we change the way that we have been perceived? Are we at a stage where we can communicate effectively with our parents and with our brothers?

sistah caroline Yeah well, unfortunately I don't live at home anymore with my parents, but I think what I did while I was there, I reiterated to my brother, that, you know, the reason why he's able to wear those running shoes on his feet, is able to go to the store and so forth, is because of my mother and the sacrifices that she has made. Unfortunately my brother sometimes needs a hard lesson, so when my mother at one point took quite ill, that's when he got scared. He's so used to having mom around, and when she wasn't around he totally lost it and so he stepped up. Like, the Hip Hop videos, he's right into that, but he's now become aware that certain terms used to describe women are not acceptable. I think he's becoming more conscious because we are older and we're doing more activities outside of the house. He sees us more like role models because we're actually working out there in the community. So I think he is stepping up, but it's a hard process. He's thirteen years old.

maxine Your little brother sounds a lot more conscious than my older brother (*laughter*), because my older brother still lives at home and still depends on my mother, and he's 22, right? He was always the king. He got to come home whenever he came home. He didn't have to do any dishes or any of that 'cause I was the girl. I had to masquerade around the house like he was some big time hot shot. I resented that, that's why I can identify with these younger sisters. I resented the fact that I was right home after school and I had to look around and see what needed to be done, and do it. He came home and if he wanted to cook something he would cook it for himself and he would use twenty pots (*laughter*) and then if my mother came home and saw the twenty pots I would get yelled at because I didn't wash them, right? And not only that, in my house the men had the power. Men sat on the couch while I had to help my mother in the kitchen and this is after she had finished her third job. She came home and she had to cook and then I got yelled at because I didn't take anything out of the fridge to thaw, right?

sistah caroline Right.

maxine I think after a while when we mature, we understand all of the reasons behind why I had to do this and why I had to do that. But there's still that kind of resentment because even now I don't like housework. I don't want to fill that kind of role, because I'm much more than how many toilets I can scrub.

host Right. And the next point is, what responsibility do you young women have? Do you have to pass this information on to your mothers? What does it mean for your mothers, in many instances, not having a male around to help them with the chores. And what is the impact of that on the male child?

sistah caroline I think a lot of times young people take their mother's history for granted. Because they're not a Sojourner Truth. You-know-what-I'm-saying? But to actually sit down and talk to your mother—I have just, over the last four years found out some stuff, family background, you know? My mother was born in Nova Scotia, my grandfather was an army brat, and she travelled all across Canada. She encountered a lot of racism in Montreal. The first time she was ever called a nigger she didn't even know what it was until sometime later. And when she came to Toronto and met with my father, he was bohemian, and there was that culture clash. It was really interesting, listening to my mother, there were so many things I learned about her that made me proud. I can tell you I would not want to be anything else than a Black woman, you-know-what-I'm-saying? I am so proud of what my mother and my foremothers did and I want to continue that for my children and my grandchildren. And I think it's important for us to sit down with our mothers and for them to tell us about their struggle, and then for us to take that and begin to tell them about how things are somewhat different for the Black women today. I think my mother, now more than ever, is really like, down with the current program, like the Hip Hop stuff that's going on and the issues surrounding that and Black women. My mother had never gone to any of my performances, and then she went to see my play 'Black Curse', and she bawled. She knew I was deep but she didn't know I was that deep, and that I had so much inside of me 'cause sometimes it's hard, you know, to talk to your mother on a certain level. But through my art I find it easier, and because she herself has a serious artistic vein she also was like, holy smokes. And I just wanna let her know that I love her very much and also my grandmother, because they are my spirit you-know-what-I'm-saying? No matter where I am, they are with me and they help me do the work I have to do.

maxine Well, you're very lucky Sistah Caroline, because I don't have that kind of relationship with my mother, but...I guess I use her as an example, her mistakes and the things she did right. Because, my mother does work very hard for what she wants, and I think I've taken that kind of philosophy to work for what I want. Nobody gives me anything, and I'm not going to rely on anybody but myself to provide for myself and to provide for my daughter.

host Marta?

marta I think that we need to look at what being female in this society means. I just read something interesting that I wanted to share.

In Maya Angelou's new book, *Wouldn't Take Nothing For My Journey Now*, she says being a woman really has nothing to do with how long you've lived. She says that just means that you've had the good luck not to be run over by a bus (*laughter*). Being a woman is very different. The experience that you go through—how you evolve and how you help people—she says that's being a woman, that's the biggest difference between being female and being a woman. And I think that mothers, daughters, sisters, we all need to unite and become women.

host   And brothers.

marta   And brothers.

sistah caroline
Yeah.

marta   So help my brothers (*laughter*). Yes, I think brothers could be helping us become equal and help us redefine ourselves and our roles.

host   How can we get our brothers to reach that level of honesty? How do we get them to understand where we're coming from?

sistah caroline   A lot of my poetry does deal with the male/female energy, and I know with my own guy, he's a wonderful man and he has come to a consciousness that we are as people both male and female, because it took those two energies to make you who you are. So, I think brothers just need to understand that they come from mothers, and that they need to sort of go into themselves and find that mother energy, so that when they look at other women they see them in the same respectable eye that they see their own mother.

maxine These are the kinds of experiences that I was talking about, issues surrounding men and women and relationships and those kinds of things. Young Black women have to deal with a lot of these issues, but because of all the conditioning in society, and all these outside things that take away a young woman's voice, we don't hear young women talk about these things. So we're asking for submissions about family, and about relationships.

host Is the book restricted to a particular age group?

maxine It's for young black women between the ages of 14 and 25.

marta I think also—talking about how brothers can help in the cause of woman empowerment, I think they have to learn to try to understand us instead of labelling us. I am very tired of being labelled. There are certain names that they call us because we do not see things in the same light, and I think, don't label me, respect me, try to understand me, and know that I am equal and that what I say is as important as what you have to say as well.

host To go back to our cultural heritage…. Of course we have differences between male and female, but our history is a bit different from the White woman.

collectively Mmmhmm.

host Because, you know, at points and times in our history we had always taken up leadership roles—even though we're taking it up—don't relegate us to a role that says 'I am supposed to be subservient.'

sistah caroline Mmmhmm.

host 'I am supposed to cater to you.' I hear from you some things such as redefining ourselves, woman empowerment, developing or creating that new spirit amongst us, so that we can forge ahead.

sistah caroline I think that a redefining of ourselves comes first from knowing ourselves, so if you don't know your history and you don't know the struggles your people have endured, you can't really begin to look at yourself and understand how you fit into that. So I think that the major thing for me and for this book, and the other contributors, is just for us to really focus on our honesty. And like I said earlier, shedding the labels, being vulnerable and in our vulnerability we will reach a higher sense of self and a higher sense of unity amongst all peoples of African descent.

host Alright...Sister Marta?

marta I also wanted to add that woman empowerment needs to come from knowing what has to be done, knowing the roles that we need to shed, being role free. Being anything that we want to be, and using empowering words, and just always noticing. Don't take everything as it says. If somebody says that you are weak, know that you are strong.

host And Sister Maxine?

maxine I think my purpose is to empower women at a younger age, you know? My younger sisters. So that by the time they are my age and older they have already found their sense of self and identity.

host Thank you all for joining me, and we look forward to **Black Girl Talk.**

Black Girl Talk thanks host, **Numvoyu Hyman**,
for forwarding this dialogue.

A Conversation with my Father

He speaks of the civil rights movement
Of Malcolm and Martin Luther
I speak of the fight for free choice
    "irrelevant"
I speak of Anita Hill
    "a traitor"
I speak of feminism
    "a ploy to drive Black men and women apart,"
    "Think of the good of the race."

And after years of listening,
I answer;
I will speak for me,
I will not be silent about your abuses,
Because it makes you look bad.
And no, I'm no traitor or sellout
I do this because I love ALL the things I am:
Black AND a woman.
And I will entreat and demand,
To be all these things
Without shame, or fear, or harm.
But never again will I be silent,
Because it makes you look bad.

susan forde

Untitled

wendy a. vincent

So this is how it feels. When the man
who promises you a rainbow lets you go.
This frigid mixture of shock and sadness.
It's so cold, so cold in here. My toes are like ice. .
My insides a gaping, empty hole. Nothing left.
All the love is gone. The meaninglessness of
late night conversations.
The futility of tender touches, secret and forbidden.
Nothing is forbidden when it's yours,
but when it never was yours,
well...

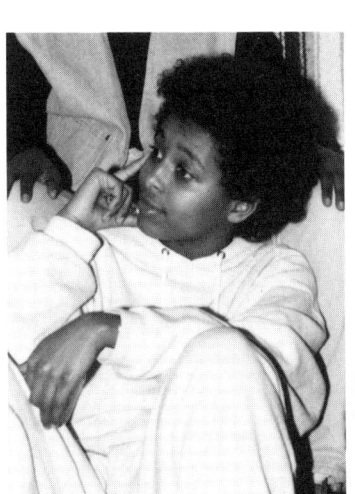

fatima jaffer

and look what the future has wrought

bob
pixie
shoulder length
braid it, french is congo, they're really the same
extend it, synthetically
brush it, 50 times not a stroke less
spray it
activate it
oil sheen it
hot comb it
chemically treat it
straighten it
perm it
texturize it
relax it (gently of course)
more like fry it
is it burning?
don't scratch
try to ignore the smell
highlight it
rinse it
dye it
permanently colour it
'til it grows out
spiral curl it
dry it with a handheld spray of hot air
moisturize it
cover it with a plastic cap
pull it back

mansa

tease it
frizz it
mousse it
gel it
hair spray it
make sure it has extra hold
hold like glue
so the curls won't droop
the style won't fade
head-band it so the roots won't show
or if it's been more than two months
you're best to cover it
or use the old trick
of handfuls of vaseline and a blowdryer
damage
breakage
split ends
conditioning treatments
olive oil, mayonnaise
placenta
super-grow formula
natural herbs
steam treatments
because we can't deviate from the norm
gotta have long, straight hair
for him to run his hands through and not get stuck
it's gotta bounce
it's gotta have body
can't look like a duplicate of him
gotta look like a woman with
hair that swings when you walk
hair that moves when you laugh
hair that he can run his hands through and not get stuck
so what will us women do next?
in our bid to maintain the norm, we really did deviate
because the norm before us,
before our mothers and even before their mothers
was kinky hair

thick hair
hair that didn't have to swing
hair that didn't have to move
hair that didn't have to have a hand go through it, unstuck
to validate its worth.

• •

My Personal Beast

erica lawson

When I was growing up, one of the things I dreaded most was having my hair washed. The experience was much like wrestling with a wild beast with strong, uncontrollable pointy tentacles reaching in all directions. Every Saturday morning, my grandmother would tame the beast by dipping it in warm water, lathering it with soap and scrubbing vigorously. The beast would recoil into thick knots but remained untamed.

I had to sit down in the sun and wait for the beast to dry, which made it more tangled and coarse to the touch. Then the war began. My grandmother raked the black teeth of the thick plastic weapon through the nappy beast, tugging and tugging while holding my small body firmly between her thighs. My head throbbed and I squealed and squirmed in pain. Slowly, cautiously, the thick nappy knots became untangled, a little bit softer. My grandmother smoothed the now-tamed beast with coconut oil, parted it in the middle, plaited both sides, tied the ends with ribbons. And set me free.

Such has been our relationship—my thick, black nappy hair and I. Over the years, I've waged many wars to tame it: I've curled it. I've permed it. I've weaved it. I've put braids in it. I've been known to throw my hands up in despair, defeated. Forced to walk around with the beast tucked firmly under a hat.

A few months ago, I told my best friend that I wanted to cut my hair and go natural. I wanted to use her as a barometer to gauge what the general reaction would be. My best friend told me, "Short, natural hair is for women who have lived a full life and are on the verge of retirement." I never raised the subject with her again. I also knew that I would have to brace myself against the snide remarks from the women in my family who worship at the altar of "good hair". I continued to suffer in silence, dreading the day when I would have to remove my braids, the last defence against the beast.

One Monday morning, after a weekend of soul-searching and recoiling at the sight of my latest set of badly-styled braids, I decided to do it. I decided to cut my hair and go natural. I ditched the braids, and made an appointment to have my hair cut. It was a scary but liberating decision.

When I arrived at the salon, I was trembling. Nervous. Was I doing the right thing? Would people still tell me that I'm pretty? Would I look like a freak?

The last thing I needed was a hair stylist to list the virtues of having my hair permed. But that's what I got. The last thing I needed was for a hair stylist to remind me that my natural hair was uncontrollable and needed a perm. But that's what she did. I asked her to give me some time to think about what I wanted to do with my hair. She handed me a pile of books with different ways of cutting and styling permed hair and told me I had twenty minutes to make a decision. As I looked at perfectly coiffured permed hair framing perfectly made-up black faces, I had serious doubts. I felt like I was turning in my membership to an established, universally-accepted beauty club. As I flipped past the beautiful, accusing faces, I was hard-pressed to find a woman with short, natural hair. As I continued to flip through the pages, my resolve strengthened. I would decide and define what I wanted to look like. I would cut my hair and go natural.

When the barber picked up his shaver, I asked him for one more minute. I took off my hat and stared at the beast for one last time. Then I watched it fall to the ground in a heap.

I now sport natural hair. And I love it.

first RIDE

The Child sat on her new dark blue bike on one side of the parking lot. She was waiting, in the dirt and tiny pebbles, for her mother (who had walked home for a drink of water), to complete a mission that her friend had accomplished the day before: to streak down Valley Avenue on her new bike without training wheels. And without falling down and skinning my side, she thought, scratching an itch on her dark brown knee. She shook the terrible thought from her head and viewed the "road" before her.

The lot, which had been filled with cars only hours before, was now deserted, leaving a long open rectangle filled with grease spots, faded yellow guidelines and notices for parents. Car tires had spread gravel and minute pieces of glass evenly around the black pavement, giving it the texture of mildly rough sandpaper. The Child's hand reached for her black ponytail and gave it a nervous tug. She stared at the large grey wall at the other end of the lot. I wish riding your bike without training wheels was as easy as getting gold stars, she thought as she looked at her rear wheel, then I wouldn't be so scared of falling down. Despite her mother's warnings, the

natalie eta

20

Child insisted her training wheels be removed only three weeks after they were attached to her bike. She felt a brief pang of fear and regret as she heard the footsteps of her trainer. Her mother, wearing her lucky red cap and lucky black sweater was holding the Child's new black and blue helmet which was bought hours before.

"Ready, honey?" she asked her daughter, handing her the helmet. The Child nodded after clipping it on.

Her mother got behind her and got a very firm grip on the seat. The Child slowly started to pedal, trying to listen to her mother's instructions and keeping her balance at the same time. She had her eyes set on the coming wall and the narrowing distance between them. When they had reached the side of the school, she smoothly turned the bicycle and started down the parking lot.

"It gets easier when you're going downhill," her mother whispered. "Pedal a bit more so you have some speed."

The Child obeyed her mother's words and the speed gradually increased. She began to hear the wind whistle past her ears. The pavement began to look uniformly black.

Suddenly, the pressure on her seat was lifted and she realized she was by herself.

"Pedal! Pedal!" Her mother's now distant voice was washed away by the sound of gravel, and the beautiful view of the fast approaching sunset.

School Daze

marta eatoru ferede

Sports? Sorry not me
Dancing?... Well I really can't
And no, my voice cannot carry a key!

Does it surprise you
That I'm here?
Well then. Let's make one thing clear...

I am here to learn what I want to do
Not to entertain the likes of you!

• •

EDUCATE

shelley rodney

'"Africa." What does that word bring to your mind, Atusha?'
'I don't know. Green forests, deserts, poor people. Momma, why do you ask?'
'Well, Atusha, you have grown up here in Connecticut since you were three. You are now sixteen years old, and you don't know nothing 'bout your past.'
'Oh, momma, please! I have books. I know all about Malcolm X, Harriet Tubman, and Martin Luther King.'
'You know what the school has taught you, and also that our ancestors were slaves. . .'
'I know all of this, mom, but what are you getting at?'
'What I'm getting at is that you need to know more. You need a full portrait of an African life, and of our culture. Now sit down and let's get busy.'
'Yo, moms, you've been watching too much Arsenio. . .'

My mother always took the time to teach me about things that would be necessary for me to know as I got older. I can't believe it's been only a year since my mother died. It seems so long. If she only knew that I haven't forgotten what she taught me. I have remembered. In heart and mind.
Now I think it is time that you should know, because. . .

> *"a people without knowledge of their past*
> *is like a tree without roots."*
> ~Anonymous~

telling it like it is

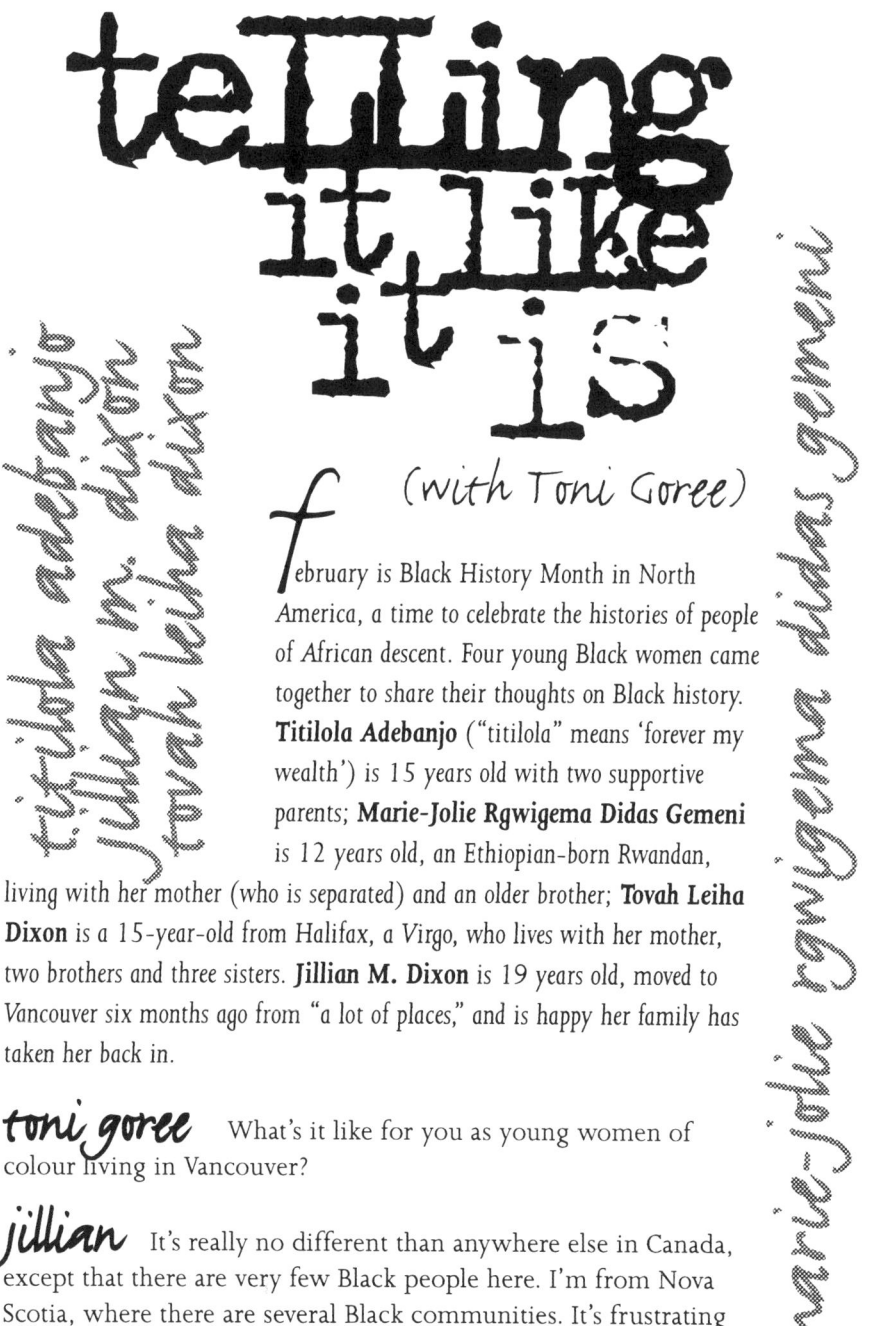

(with Toni Goree)

titilola adebanjo   jillian m. dixon   tovah leiha dixon

marie-jolie rgwigema didas gemeni

february is Black History Month in North America, a time to celebrate the histories of people of African descent. Four young Black women came together to share their thoughts on Black history. **Titilola Adebanjo** ("titilola" means 'forever my wealth') is 15 years old with two supportive parents; **Marie-Jolie Rgwigema Didas Gemeni** is 12 years old, an Ethiopian-born Rwandan, living with her mother (who is separated) and an older brother; **Tovah Leiha Dixon** is a 15-year-old from Halifax, a Virgo, who lives with her mother, two brothers and three sisters. **Jillian M. Dixon** is 19 years old, moved to Vancouver six months ago from "a lot of places," and is happy her family has taken her back in.

toni goree What's it like for you as young women of colour living in Vancouver?

jillian It's really no different than anywhere else in Canada, except that there are very few Black people here. I'm from Nova Scotia, where there are several Black communities. It's frustrating here. I work with these white people who don't understand me.

When we talk about having unlearning racism workshops, they say 'okay' but then they want me—the person of colour—to take on organizing the workshops.

tovah It's pretty difficult for me, because nobody sees me as a woman of colour—I'm light-skinned. People think I have an advantage, but I don't see it that way. I was raised by my mom who's Black and I know what it's like for her. When we lived in Pictou County where there are lots of racist White people, I was a "Nigger". But when I go to places where there are only Black people, they think I'm not Black, I'm White.

Even though I'm Mixed, people treat me differently. When I walk down the hall, the guys say, "Whoomp, there it is," meaning my butt, and I hate it. They say that to me because they know I'm Black. They would never say that to a White girl.

It's also weird with the girls. White girls will touch my hair and say, "it's like you're hair's got grease in it, yuck." Black Girls will say, "You don't got to put nothin' in your hair girl, you got nice hair, your hair isn't all that kinky." But that makes me feel like people are trying to deprive me of who I am.

marie Vancouver's a lot different from where I used to live too. I was born and raised in Ethiopia, and everybody was Black there, so who are we going to be racist to? I've met with a lot of racism in Canada, even stupid little comments thrown in whenever people insult me. They always seem to make it about my race, no matter what.

It happens to my brother too. My brother was trying to break up a fight between a guy and some kid on the bus, and the guy says, "Shut up, you stupid little nigger." My brother started fighting him and ended up getting community service for that, yet absolutely nothing happened to the White guy.

titi Even though I was born in Vancouver, I have to deal with the fact that there aren't enough Black people here. School is hard because I don't know how people will take it when I say, "Can we do a report on Black History Month?" They think it's only for Black people and that I'm being racist against them. I have to keep forcing myself to speak up because if I don't tell them about it, who will? I'm the only Black person in the class.

toni   Why is Black History Month important to you?

jillian   In Nova Scotia, it meant a lot of things happening, at the libraries for example. Black History Month means a big celebration of just being a Black person—more than during the rest of the year. The culture is so specific and special and the people are great. But it doesn't seem to mean a whole lot in Vancouver. In the future, I'm going to try and make it mean something to other people.

tovah   Black History Month is important to me, because my mother taught me about Black History all my life. It's just as much a part of me as my body. I also think it's important because Black people have endured so much, and have achieved greater things than any White man, because they had to rise above people putting them down.

I want to teach people my history. I want to say, "Yeah, Black people created what you're wearing. A Black person created that." If I said a Black person, or a person of colour built the CN Tower, you'd question it and say, "How do you know? Are you sure?" If someone said a White man built the CN Tower you'd just go, "Yeah." White people totally want to deny the fact that maybe a Black man could do so-and-so.

Black History Month is also important because it's a time when we can set things straight. And so when my little brother grows up, he won't have to feel uncomfortable in class about raising his hand. Even I feel weird about raising my hand and telling the teacher it was a Black man, not a White man, who did that. It's not my job to correct the teacher, but if I don't, nobody in the school will.

marie   I feel we should all know about Black history. We don't learn it in school and nobody cares about it. But I care so I want to know. Black History Month itself is kind of meaningless because nobody pays any regard to it. I learn as much as I can because my mom teaches me and I read books. I want to know about my ancestors and I want to know about everything we've been through. I want to know about who I am, what I've been and what I'll be.

titi   Black history is important because of all the things we've achieved.

There are so many things I don't know about my history, and so much I need to know about our struggles. I was reading about Rosa Parks, and the fact that she had to go to jail because she said, "No, I won't move to the back of the bus." (Segregation laws in the U.S. required Black people to sit at the back of the bus.) People don't seem to understand that Black History Month isn't just for Black people. It's a way for us all to come together despite the history of slavery, and because going through slavery has traumatized the race.

If there was no such thing as Black History Month, I probably wouldn't be able to talk about Martin Luther King and Rosa Parks and all those people, and I probably wouldn't have any self-respect, or knowledge that I can achieve so-and-so too. The fact that those people had the courage to say, "I'm a human being too. I have a heart and a mind like anyone else"—that gives me courage too.

I learned the other day that a Black man was the first world explorer to get to the Antarctic. A White man got the credit for it and the Black guy became a clerk or something. The books he wrote were largely unsold. If it wasn't for the fact that I'm doing a report this year on Black History Month, I probably wouldn't have heard of him.

tovah   I want to add that while it's hard to be Black, it's hell to be a Black woman. You get double the pressure. If we do get to learn Black history, we're probably going to learn about the men first. I want it to come closer to home, to learn about Black women's history. I can relate better to a Black woman because my mom is one.

It's important to me, as a young person, to see how my mother made it—she had a child at 15 and then kept having children. Now I'm 15 and go to school; I've got a home. If she could make it, I can make it even better. It's like I'm living my mom's dream—not that I have to live up to her standards, but she made me set goals and showed me she could do it, that I am her daughter and am strong just like her.

titi   The fact that schools don't teach anything about Black people pisses me off. I know more about White history, which has little to do with me. I don't give a damn about Christopher Columbus because he did not discover this country—it belonged to the First Nations people. I don't think we should be taught about Columbus in school. There's this stereotype about us, especially in the media, that Black people are criminals, they have babies at a young age, they don't know how to take care of them... If teachers talk about Black people, it's in one sentence: "They were slaves." They don't mention the struggles and pain these people had to go through, or tell the real story of what happened, how people were crowded together in the ships as if they were animals.

I'm not saying we should only have Black history, but the history is not complete. They talk about the colonists, about how the Aboriginal peoples were slaves first, then Black people were. But then they beat around the bush and don't get specific. If you want to talk about history, bring up everything. If they don't teach Black and Native History in school, I'm not being fully educated.

jillian I quit school two years ago because I couldn't deal with the pressure, I didn't like the teachers and the way they treated me. This was in Halifax. There were Black people at school, but the teachers were White.

About 90 percent of the students didn't finish the year. I was in high school for two years in Halifax, and I met maybe two Black kids who had graduated. Everyone just wants to hang out in the cafeteria and party, and the principal doesn't stop you and say, "Go to class." He doesn't care if you graduate. It's got nothing to do with his pay cheque.

We fought for a year to get a Black History course put into the curriculum. When we finally got it, we were so happy, everyone signed up for it—but you needed a grade 12 English credit to get in. Then we found out it wasn't a Black History course, but a regular English course that would sometimes use books by Black authors. In early January, I asked friends in Halifax how the class was going, and they hadn't read anything by a Black author yet.

Now they have a Black guidance counsellor at each of the high schools who's supposed to be from the 'hood' and be able to control his own people. He's the only one there to keep us down—there are a lot of riots and stuff like that, and kids will skip off school to go to other schools and cause trouble. Sure it's stereotypical stuff, but they don't teach you anything and until they do, I ain't going back.

tovah I don't feel like I'm learning what I want to be taught, what I feel I have the right to be taught. I know I need the basics, but I also need to feel

I can go further. A lot of White girls and boys graduate—they know their history. They can say, "Mom, I learned about so-and-so today, he's our cousin or whatever way back." I don't want to learn about that anymore. I know they're the ones who colonized. Okay, I get it! They try to convince me that white people are number one. I'm not convinced.

I want to learn something about me now, or about that girl across the room who's not Black nor White. I want to learn how they cook food, how they lived way back in pre-historic times, what they did. That's history. That's what's going to make me be fascinated by this course, what intrigues me and makes me want to know more. Learning about Hudson's Bay just kills it for me.

Today when they talk about Nova Scotia in the school system, it's about fishing, about Peggy's Cove—they make it seem like everybody in Halifax goes to the Harbour every Sunday to fish. It's not like that. They don't talk about the race riots, or the fact that Halifax was the first place in Canada that Black people ever settled. When I tell the teacher I want to learn Black History, I don't want to hear that we were slaves: I know that. I want to know about our achievements, what goals we set.

Half the school is made up of non-White cultures. It might spark something in us if we learned about different cultures. Maybe then we'd get more Native kids and kids of colour graduating instead of just White kids.

Today a friend and I went to the teacher and said, "We want a petition asking for Black studies and multicultural studies. Will you help us?" The teacher said yes. I looked at him and thought, "Oh my God, that was easy." But I know it was luck. I know the next step is going to be even harder just by the way he said yes.

We feel we're the only ones who want things to change, but it's not true. When I went to school, my friend Leah said, "I want a petition. I don't feel that I'm learning enough." Then I go home and my brother is talking to my mom and doesn't know I'm listening and he says,"Mom, I want to learn some Black history. I want to start a petition." It's in us all, but we never talk about it because we're never asked.

I think our parents have really strong kids, because we're not leaving it up to other people and we're not saying, "When we're 20, we'll try to do something for Black History Month." We're all teenagers here in this room. At first, I thought this project was just for Kinesis, but when I went back to school, I noticed people really want action. My friends want to learn about this stuff. That makes me say, "Tovah, you gotta go girl, you gotta do it!"

marie There are no Black teachers at my school, no one I can relate to, because everybody at my school is White. I'm getting an education, but not one I want. I want to know who did this, who did that, where, when, but all I learn, in social studies for example, is about European explorers.

titi I am studying about explorers, too, right now. The thing that's weird is that they get further from being "pure" White, there's less information. The teachers say education is going to get more complicated (if we change things). In other words, we're going to be learning more new things. Look how long Black history has been around—since the beginning of time. But I only started learning about it two years ago.

jillian A Black woman came to our school once, and she told us a bunch of things and brought up a good point. They teach you about the evolution theory, and the scientific theory where something exploded somewhere, but they don't teach you about the Black Woman Theory—that everyone evolved from one Black woman in Africa, and as you moved farther north and south and east and west, you lost pigment in your skin due to the climate and environment. That sounds far more realistic than evolution or something blowing up in space or Adam and Eve. It's closer to home for me. But they don't talk about it, not even in religious studies.

titi   It's like that with anything to do with places that are considered "Third World Countries". These are basically places that were either stolen from or invaded. People say, "Oh, they're all poor," et cetera. It's a put down. I feel if I went to a Third World country, I'd probably learn about so many backgrounds and histories and amazing achievements that you'd never learn about here.

People also say Canada's a free place where you can have respect and can speak your mind. If you can speak your mind, why isn't Black History being taught? Why can't we learn these things about ourselves?

marie   I used to live in Ethiopia and they consider that a Third World country. Whenever I speak to people about Ethiopia, they ask me questions like, "Were you starving there?" I wasn't starving! I lived. People ask me what kind of a house I lived in: "Was it a dirty shack?"

They have this idea of what each place in the world is like, but they don't really know. Even if it was like that, people here wouldn't know that it's because the White people came, colonized it, kept things for themselves and then left everything in a big mess. People think we did that, probably because we're lazy or we never work. It's absolutely not true.

tovah   It goes back to White people teaching the history. That's why nobody knows anything about any other culture. Let's teach our own history and then it'll get taught right. I always question my social studies book because I know White men wrote all the textbooks. Nowadays, it's getting a little better, people of colour are writing the occasional book.

My mother told me the other day that Beethoven was Black, he ain't White. So in class I say, "He's White in this picture, but he ain't White in the picture I saw yesterday." They say, "Well, I didn't know that. We'll talk about it later after class." I want to say, "No, we won't!" You try to scare the teachers and they get scared because they don't know what you know.

titi   A lot of people get really nervous around Black people. We had a substitute teacher this month and she was talking about Black people and Africa. Then she noticed I was in the class. She started stuttering as if she had forgotten her language: "Um, okay, well, Black people in um Africa..." and I'm thinking, "What is she um talking ah...about?"

If I have a question, they act like I'm trying to put them down, like I'm trying to say that maybe they don't know better, that they shouldn't be a teacher. But that's their problem. I think my question deserves to be answered. I want to know if they feel it was a White person who did so-and-so, and I want to know what their source for that is. I have to talk about the media again. They always name three or four countries in Africa where people are all starving. A country, never mind a continent, is a big place. They never tell you anything else about that country. Starvation is going on here in Canada too, but it doesn't mean it's happening to everyone.

People here learn one little fact about a certain people and think that's the way it is for everybody. Maybe a few Black people have an attitude problem—and they'll say all Black people have attitudes. When people meet me, they say, "I used to think you were like all those Black girls that have major attitude." And what if I do have an "attitude?" If I get mad, I might start doing the hand thing but that's just a way of expressing yourself, like slang or a figure of speech.

tovah People always make fun of me in class, especially when I talk about Black History Month, because I get really mad. So when I have a question to ask, like today when I asked the teacher about the petition, I mumbled and couldn't talk any louder. Now, I think I have a nice, big, strong voice, so I felt like I was looking up to my teacher and it made me mad.

I got tears in my eyes, I was so angry. They expect us to throw things around, but when they don't teach Black history, when they say something or disregard what I say, it makes me want to get up and headbutt them or something. Instead, I turn red and start shaking. The most I can do is stare down the teacher and try to mess him up when he's talking.

toni As young Black women, how do you feel about your opportunities and future?

titi I feel like if I want to get opportunities—actually be accepted in this world and achieve things—I have to do it for myself. You have to say, "Okay, I'll do my math homework." You can't say, "I'll do it tomorrow." Your future becomes what you make of the present.

As a young Black woman, I feel I have to work harder than someone who isn't Black. I get good grades in school, but if I did one thing wrong, it would seem like all that reputation I built up since I was a kid would be gone. They'd say, "Oh, she's just one of those Black people that are on the streets and doing all those crimes." Yet there are so many people committing crimes who aren't Black; most of them are White. They know that, but they have this idea that all White people are smart and created all that stuff and did all those things.

I'll have to work hard to make a future for myself, because it's hard right now and I don't know how it's going to be in a couple of years. Black people are getting used to the fact that we need to know about ourselves and, once you've realized that, you can go further. We've come such a long way, but we have to keep on going.

marie Being a young Black woman is the toughest thing to be because we have to put up with men and with people who are racist towards us. It's a man's world and a White person's world too. When you're a Black person and a woman, people are always looking for some reason not to include you in something. You've always got to do your best to be on top. If a White person and I were going for the same job, I know they'd look for some reason to hire the White person, because that happens to my mother. The people who have all the power up there are White men.

But I'm going to do whatever I want to. I feel being a young Black woman makes me want to work all the harder. I want to get somewhere, and I want every other Black woman to rise above everything. People put hurdles for us to go over, and I'm going over them.

tovah I feel I have a long road ahead of me, just like any other woman of colour has. It's not all about White people; there's Black against Black, White against Hispanic against Black. There is a lot of racism. And we may be Black women but we are women first.

I know I have a future, that's there's something out there waiting for me because I can tell—everyday when I go to school or look in the mirror, I look at myself and say, "You're going to go somewhere, you're going to be a somebody, don't worry." As long as I've got my family behind me and my mother ahead to guide me, I don't feel I have anything to worry about.

I think the worst part is already over—being young and having to go through some of the stuff I've been through. I'm a strong person and I'll make a future for myself. I'm going to try and do it all. I don't get the best grades and I'm not the best person, but I'm human just like everybody else. I can overcome great obstacles just like everybody else. I think my future's pretty bright.

jillian There's not a lot of opportunities for me as a youth. No one takes me seriously. Being a young Mixed Race woman, I've fallen into all the stereotypes I could have: I dropped out of school; I've fooled around; I only got a grade 10 education; I've gotten pregnant; I've gotten on welfare; I moved out when I was 16. All these things are due to not getting enough support at school, or at home—though my mom tried so hard, I couldn't listen to what she had to say, I had to learn for myself.

I'm going to be 19 soon and right now, the future doesn't look so bright because I feel I have to go back a couple of steps. But I've got high hopes. I've got a job for the first time and I have been there five months. I've got clothes. I'm enrolled in school. I'm overcoming a lot of the hurdles that I fell off before.

A big thank-you to Lynn MacKinlay and Agnes Huang for their time and good humour, for driving and for providing snacks and to Toni Goree for facilitating the interview. Thanks also to Sur Mehat for hours of transcribing.

sporting Womanhood

joi-elle dinnall

there is a satisfying truth

That quenches me

Even in moments of solitude

Picture me simplicity

Wild like heather on the moors

Sleek and finished

Bold, with edges sure

Knowing I am all these things

I remain soothing, powerful, calm

Drenched in basic bliss

A Miss igniting energies

Marching to her beat

Willing you to be equally rich

My gift to you is this…

when i taste the love

anna bauer

When I taste the love that breathes from you

It subdues me in a sweet oblivion

Drowned, I gaze from the bottom through sparkling crystals

And reach up

To touch your face

Lick your lips

Savour your flavour

And swallow you

Ethereal we rise

A strengthened being

Potent so holy

Guard me, I'll shelter you

We've submitted and accepted the fate of the divine

A Black Woman's Haiku

lisa hollingsworth

Chocolatey, smooth and
handsome is the black man on
my mind, yum…yum…yum.

david zapparoli

NAKED

i
barely
breathing
lay tightly curled up in a hard ball
no passage for even a fine ray of light
beyond the reach of passionate love
that same wonder
for which I patiently yearn

That which would slowly,
ever so gently,
peel away those callous layers
and glide
against the inner trembling flesh
shedding fear like large petals
of a single, lonely flower
igniting that warm, moist orifice
with thrusts of passion

A sensation of acute measure
pierces the core
one final
hot thrust
heat so intense

karen lee

shatters the aged shell
as it explodes
so does my pleasure
in a moment of sheer ecstasy

Juices of once hindered lust
now spill freely
splashing shards
of my former enclosure
with it flows intense pain
which until that moment
remained imprisoned

Warm wetness spills
covering my flesh
in a light sheet of peace
a wide smile
spreads slowly across my face
as I lay,
wide open
no longer bound
by coats of sadness
wounds sheared away

I
glistening
with wet beads of joy
naked
at peace
at last.

DARK berry

charmaine lewis

Someone has caused us to collide
You exiting the moving masses of flesh
Swaying to the music, me trying to enter it

My arms move out to steady you
And i felt the soft, moist silkiness of your
sweat covered skin

In that moment that i brushed against you
I felt your heartbeat and i inhaled your scent
Which brought to mind a bowl of fresh fruit
On a hot summers day

We smiled and i looked into your eyes
What do they reflect when you are aroused?
Your teeth were like the white keys
of a brand new piano

I WONDER WHAT YOUR SEX LOOKS LIKE?

Your skin is dark and smooth
To be exact the colour is nut brown
Your eyes remind me of 2 twinkling stars
in the dead of night

The moisture on your face reflects
the flashing lights and
I wonder what it would be like to run
my tongue over that moisture

I ASK YOU A QUESTION?

I watch your mouth as your tongue protrudes
through the corner of your lip
Which is tinged with some warm color
My mind wanders as your lips move rhythmically
to form words that answer my questions

WHAT DOES YOUR SEX LOOK LIKE?

Is your clit hard and demanding poking
through those 2 lips
Which are surrounded by a bush of dark
leaves glistening with dew
What would it be like to kiss those lips
and have you move to my music

What would it be like to touch those 2 lips
and run my fingers through your valley
To be taken over by the sweet musky odour
To get lost in the darkness of you

You make a move to depart from me
and i realize
that all i have to remember you by is
your tongue protruding from the corner
of your lips tinged in some warm color

2 BODIES 1 LOVER

*t*wo bodies entwined with a passionate force —
Tongues lashing, arms clutched,
Skin on skin, sweat dripping.
The taste — sweet
The feel — oh so tender
— oh so gentle.
Hands full of strength and desire
Moving this way and that —
Sliding up and down backs, thighs, lips, eyes.
What once was a lustful sight
Has grown into a beautiful, meaningful,
Making of love.
None wanting the end to near
None wanting the bodies to part
None wanting the moon to fall
None wanting the sun to rise.
Two bodies — entwined with a passionate force.

lorraine anne mcleod

inteRluDe

With Open heart
And Open legs
She took Him
His tattooed breath
The warmth of her body
He stood before her
A Black Sun
To her Indigo Sky
Lips that tangle in a dance
as old as time
Yet he gives nothing but
a martyred kiss
To her dying love
His velvet skin
The night sky
To dance her dance
Of Wanton Lust
A tongue encapsulates
Thoughts
Rhythm
Texture
Glides easily on smooth skin
He closes his eyes
And breathes her
Hand over nipple
Legs interlock
He rides easy
Deep in the saddle
Of her Ebony Back

nicole minerve

Pears Of green & yellow

*r*ipen avocado
Rolls through
My eager tongue.

Light
Salty cream
Sliding in
Heavy
Base
Tempo
Drums
Deep.
Into the depths of my
Salivating oneness.

Now
I am in shelter
In solace.
I feel the Goddess.
My wholeness
And the pleasure
She has ordained for me.

camille bailey

Your broken starvation
Invades
My sensations.

Come
I'll let you enter
My avocado scenes.

Come
Let me
Glide my fingers
Through your
Butter salty creams

In green
We'll meet the Goddess
And feed
On Yellow
Ecstasy.

rose-anne bailey

York? hoMos? REALLY?

maxine greaves

My first few weeks at York were filled with excitement, anxiety and dreams—everything that I was supposed to feel about starting a new school, starting university. I kept to myself, mostly because I didn't know anybody, but also because I had just come out as a lesbian and I was scared to death that someone would recognize and expose me.

Don't get me wrong—I was afraid, not anti-social. I made friends. I was even approached by the members of certain organizations for Black youth at York University. Actually, I couldn't turn around or scratch my ass without having someone give me a lecture on the importance of my support for my brothers in the community, and the importance of Black unity on campus (although these organizations have yet to find a way to be unified).

Maybe if I hadn't just come out I would have challenged these questions like: "Really?... Now tell me, what does your organization have to offer me, a strong, intelligent, grassroots, conscious, womyn identified, pussysuckin' sistah, fresh out of high school? This young Black woman carrying her own ideologies on how this world should be run, how she wants to be known and how she wants to be heard? How is your organization going to support me, when my brothers and sisters want to dismiss my contribution to the struggle and divorce themselves from me and my realities as a Black woman, a Black lesbian? When will your organization acknowledge my existence and the existence of other lesbians in OUR community?"

I'm sure I would have asked those kinds of questions if I was confronted now with those lectures, but then I was still green like springtime, so instead

I just stood listening. Instead, I just stood trying to figure out ways to inconspicuously get from the food court to the Womyn's Centre. I had been warned that it was the 'gay club' by a young woman who was so afraid of lesbians that the thought of me simply touching the doorknob sent her running in a frenzied panic. This was the only womyn and lesbian positive space in the school that I had found, not for lack of looking, but I was scared to breeze in and out as I pleased, 'cause hey, this ain't my bedroom... this is York.

It ain't like I can say to a brother "Yeah, I know what you mean...Black womyn are the most beautiful womyn in the world. We have womyn that swim in the deepest oceans of blue black ebony to womyn luminous with the light of the full moon, all the womyn in between, the chestnut browns, the deep mahoganies, the almond browns, the honey brown and lustrous golds. Sweet and alluring, wise and discerning, carrying the words and whispers of our ancestors in her womb and her hair, on her lips and on her mind. OH...yes my brother...I know the beauty of my sisters...I know why you are so enchanted by their voices, because they ring with the voices of our grandmothers...why you are enamoured by their eyes, because they hold the memories of the people we once were, and why you are captivated by their minds, because they remember a knowledge bestowed by the Seven African Orishas."

Those are words that I could never utter to a brother as a sister loving sistah—he would just act like he didn't know what I meant!

It's sad. Here we are five hundred years later, still oppressed and repressed, still having to search for our lost selves, asking the very people who stole our identity, Who are we? Looking to this Eurocentric society for answers they could never, and would never, give to us. Here we are, people in need of each other. We are willing to divide ourselves into smaller, weaker units, more manageable, less threatening, less likely to become anything more than ghetto hounds and crack babies (at least that is what we've been taught. Don't believe me? Pick up the next issue of the *Toronto Sun*).

I am a Black lesbian. I am willing to work, organizing in the name of my people; I live to better my communities. I will do all I can to ensure that our children find their voices, so they can speak their minds and find their strength so nobody can take their voices away. I am a sistah who loves women. I will no longer remain invisible to my own.

going WITHOUT

for the woman who makes my clit dance

Withdrawal from sex
causes brain damage
believe me
it's been proven

2 mths without
deep, passionate,
    heart-in-mouth
    love-you-forever
    want-you-now
kissing, causes the
nose to rot
and eventually
fall off

*and no one wants
anyone
with a gaping hole
in the middle of their
face

going to long
without
sensual
all over body
massages

that end in steaming
tongue baths

is bad for the heart
and can actually
stop it from beating

again,
check the statistics
it's been proven

going without
the feel of another's
probing, wet tongue
on your throbbing
aching
clit
can cause blindness
and clit failure
a condition that renders
the clit useless,
as it becomes
absolutely unresponsive
to stimulus
note *this condition
can be reversed only through

suzanne anderson

prolonged sessions
of
finger/tongue/teeth/clit-to-clit
sucking, fucking, teasing, pleasing
external stimuli
from a woman you love
or a reasonable fac simile

so,
what i'm trying to say is:

you need every inch
of my body
to prevent your brain
from degenerating
into nothingness

you need my fingers
      my tongue
      my teeth
      my fist
      my clit
against yours
to prevent clit failure

and you need my need
      my desire
      my lust
      my love
for you

to make it all
worthwhile

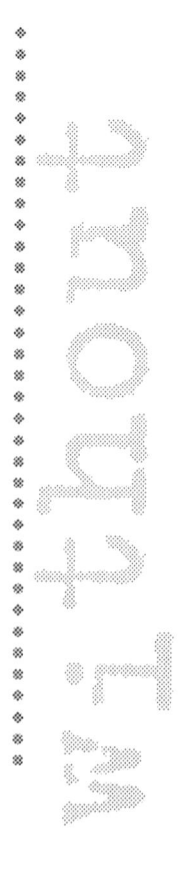

With Out You

stacey ringle

With out you I'm nothing
With out you I'm lost
With out you I can't breathe
With out you I can't feel
        Touch
        Caress
With out you I can't love
        Care
        Adore
        Or
        Fantasize
With out you I can't possibly go on
I need you
I love you
And you've shown me in more ways than
One, that I have you.
No lover, it's not you but, my sweet
Saviour   Jah, Rastafari.

        Peace out!

normal people

ayoka silvera

i was always afraid of falling into the gap. To me it seemed like the gaping maw of some nasty beast. I thought of the train as the monster's silver tongue, come to receive all the people on its palate and roll them down its throat. Now as I stand in the dirty subway car, remembering my illusions, I just have to laugh out loud. I listen to the echoes of my mirth down the tunnel.

I feel their eyes on me, making a scene. I try to ignore them, but the tension becomes too much. My brother always told me, "Confront rudeness with rudeness". I turn and fix the Marlboro Man with my stony gaze. I then confront the winking woman on the Eatons poster; the smug anchorman on the CBC ad; the Certs couple with the cheesy grins. I sense them all shuddering inwardly—this satisfies me.

I realized very early that because they cannot smell or touch anything, the people in the posters are watchers. At that time I harboured the ridiculous notion that they could suck my very essence from me if I made extended eye contact. Oh, what a foolish child I was. It took me a good ten years to get over my subway fears and it still makes me shudder when I feel their mocking stares.

The other people on the car stare too, but to experience their gaze is not so harrowing. I know they stare because of the deformity.

I walk to a seat. It is not empty, but it soon will be. The jean-clad young woman looks me up and down for a few seconds before she suddenly stands and walks to the other end of the car. I take my seat and settle in. Lydia, my "silent partner", is with me, but then she is always with me, isn't she. Her tongue never developed fully so doesn't talk, but she certainly takes up a lot of space. Normally, I would have to squeeze to make head room for her. Instead, the people on both sides of me get up and leave, just as I expect them to. I'm not malodorous or sick looking. It is because of the deformity that people stay away from me.

Everyone stares at me; children; women; men; young; old; rich or poor. I guess I'm an equal opportunity spectacle.

When I am not eyeing the posters on the subway I watch my audience, even though I know it is rude to stare. Both Lydia and I stare them down—well, Lydia doesn't really see very much because her eyes never opened completely when she was born, but I gawk at the gawkers with as much curiosity as they feel for me. I try to gauge from their reactions what it is like to be normal, yet get stared at. Most all of them are unsettled by my gaze, as if I were Medusa, but once, a middle-aged man sat by me. He asked my name and whether I'd like to have tea with him that night. Poor Lydia never gets asked out, but I had no time for pity. I jumped at the chance to be with this man. I spent that evening dressing and changing, trying to find the perfect look. Even though it is impossible for me to look like the women in magazines, I get as close as I can. It turned out he was just looking for recruits for his travelling side show. I left his apartment in tears.

Oh, it's my stop. I get up and do the most embarrassing thing. As I give the people on the car the customary bow, Lydia hits her head on a seat. Not only am I humiliated but I just know I will have a migraine this evening. The trouble with having two heads is that we feel each other's mishaps, doubling the pain. Well, c'est la vie. I shuffle off of the train holding my heads and go home.

Hurt

the sound would sing out over the playground
Fight fight a nigger and a white
Fight fight a nigger and a white

As my stomach knotted
I knew this involved me
How could it not
When my brother and I were the only black kids in the school

Fight fight a nigger and a white
I ran to where the crowd had started to group
I could barely see
I did know that in the centre of everything
There was one black kid
My brother

They kept yelling
Fight fight a nigger and a white
But he was alone
It was them, all of them, not just the one
Against him

The friends he did have said nothing
Just standing, waiting, watching
Fight fight a nigger and a white

This had nothing to do with kids stuff
That maybe they got in fight over the swings
Or that they just didn't like each other
The chant said it all
Fight fight a NIGGER and a white
It was about the colour of their skin

tara darrall

Nothing more, nothing less
Fight fight a nigger and a white
Such a young age, and they already knew what it was about

I looked at my brother carefully
He had his stance ready
He wasn't going to back down
He was a strong kid
But his eyes were aching
He didn't want to do this
But he had no other choice
Fight fight a nigger and a white

Only I knew my brother well enough to know
What was in his eyes
It was not hardness or indifference
That the others may see

I had seen and felt the love and gentleness in his eyes
I had felt the warmth of his hand wrapped around my own
Not the clenched fist, now stiff at his side
My brother's entire body screamed of hurt
But only I heard his scream above the chant
Fight fight a nigger and a white

Still today the hurt exists
Not the hurt of the fight
At ten years old, fists can only do so much damage

The hurt is from having everyone against him
For the colour of his skin
Fight fight a nigger and a white

Talking back in CLASS

valery mendus

a white face. A White woman's face. It smiles at me, a commercialized gesture intended to welcome commuters on the TTC. She is wearing construction clothing. I suppose another decision made in the Advertising Department, a decision 'they' felt would deflect gender stereotypes about women. A wise decision they concluded, considering the progressive attitude of the times. Besides, a society burning in a furious ideological climate is best cooled, according to the code of media protection, by 'political correctness'. No matter. I notice her seemingly sincere twinkling eyes embraced by lying lines that blow her cover. My searching eye abandons the false security of her lying expression, trace down her plastic white face, over her 'like new', workman's clothing, and the pretentious toolbox-prop in her right hand to come face-to-face with the bold red print at the bottom of the poster, "RIDE THE ROCKET". TTC.

RIDE THE ROCKET AND GET TAKEN FOR A RIDE. My mind quickly is reminded of the events that have occurred this morning, January 17, 1995. I had boarded the Scarborough 86A bus, headed for Kennedy Station, bus number 6715 to be exact. It was just after 12:00 p.m., I was late for school, as usual. My child was delighting in the fact of how lucky we were today to get to take the bus vs. the car. I was sitting near the front entrance, humoured by the innocence of childhood, the blind trust children award undeserving adults, the simple beauty they attribute to an undeserving world...

A young woman steps onto the bus. She is engulfed in thick baggy dark-coloured clothing, her petite head swallowed by a BIG, BLACK hungry Gangsta' toque. Her 2-inch-thick, bracelet-size gold hoop earrings hang oddly from her famished toque and causes one to assume her face is intended to accessorize her earrings, rather than the other way around. She wears no make-up and her infant eyes peep out from the straight, blank face, concealing her story. She makes her way to the back of the bus, where only the rough tough and proud can take domain, her tall, slim frame shuffled by her smooth sure manly strut. She stops at the beacon, shifts and returns to the driver, then continues to strut to the back of the bus, her expression bothered only by an uplifted angry brow overlooking the ridge of her face. Her black face. Her young black face. Her young, poor, hip-hop-gear-wearing face.

Suddenly the bus swerves, to my surprise and discomfort, and my child cries out, "Mommy, why are we stopping?" In a split second, I, too, demand to know—yes, why has the bus stopped? My questioning and irritated glance strikes the ice-blue-eyed, white-haired, white-faced driver, who replies to my unspoken question by booming a thunderous demand over the P.A. System that the student show her card or the bus will not move. The 'student' is constant, she is unwavering, she simply replies, "I have all day."

I am ashamed to say that almost immediately I felt outraged, my impatience inflamed, my accusing eyes dismissing the driver and settling comfortably on the forehead of this presumptuous person who has stopped the bus, robbing my time, inconveniencing my day. "Why doesn't SHE show her card. SHE probably doesn't even have one, or SHE probably has a card that doesn't belong to her. Or SHE doesn't have enough money to pay the fare…" My crucifying thoughts are interrupted by the supervisor's authoritative voice over the still bus, silent with noisy, furious contemplation. "THIS IS THE SUPERVISOR. THE STUDENT MUST SHOW HER STUDENT CARD IMMEDIATELY. FAILURE TO DO SO MAY INVOLVE POLICE INTERVENTION AND INCONVENIENCE OTHER TTC PATRONS." Still, she moveth not. I am getting more and more angered by such injustice, such ignorance, such attitude… Who does she think she is? Rosa Parks-wanna-be? Just show the man the damn card, so we all can go.

Like as though the condescending faceless order was a signal to attack, each TTC 'patron' lets their eyes fall on the 'student', their stares burdening her brow, one on top of the other, reaching a climax, stimulated by a low muttering, until suddenly, a middle-aged West Indian Black man sharply turns his head and literally jumps all over the girl with his screams. "What is your problem?! You are a coloured person. You know they always give us trouble—you are coloured—what do you expect? You know they wouldn't give you this problem if you were a White girl. Now show the man your card—You are embarrassing all the coloured people on the bus! Show him now!" Still she moveth not, but her eyes reveal her startled heart. A Black someone flatly states, "You're not embarrassing me—You're embarrassing yourself!" A fair-skinned, young Hip-Hopish Black guy speaks for the 'student'. He angrily shouts back at the man, "You know it's unfair, it's 'cause she's Black and you think that she should lie back and take this shit?!" They both stand up and bark at each other. We 'coloured' folk anticipate a fight. (Everyone on the bus is Black or Indian—There are only three White people). My child fearfully cries, "What's going on mommy?"

I look around, well, well, well—it seems the classroom is in an uproar. The kids are quarreling because Miss Thang won't go to her desk and until she does the whole class has to stay in for recess, their teacher has conveniently reminded them. I glance back at the teacher, I mean driver, and hear him mutter, "I'm not taking this crap from 'those' people or anyone! I'll get the police." My ear pulls my face around in response to a white face. A White woman's white face. It cries, "If you don't like it, go back where you came from." A courageous ignition to an argumentative fire, that I, too, find myself burning in. "What the hell do you mean by that, lady? Shut up!—you have no right to say that—you're an immigrant yourself."

The Driver, Mr. Blue Eyes, suddenly is overcome by a wave of panic at the thought of a race riot, and the potential of physical harm to his white body. He commands us all off the bus, it is out of service, and like school children, we exit the vehicle. Unfortunately, he has made no provision for his school children. Three buses have passed us by. He could soon call for 'assistance', but couldn't call for another bus for his inconvenienced, poor, dark, patrons.

Like a bird dragging a broken wing, I struggle to my destination, my child, my bag, her bag and my frustration in hand. I've assumed that SHE, the student, like many, has monopolized on racism at my expense. You know, those people who do things ass-way around and then plead 'RACISM' when there are repercussions. But as I make my way back to the next bus stop, my fury calming, insight starts to ooze down my brain like thick molasses, and I start to wonder if, in fact, this was a racist incident. It's true, whether the student was right or wrong, she would not have been given such a hassle at everyone's expense, if she had, perhaps, looked like Mr. Driver's daughter, very blond, very bluish-eyed, very 'clean-cut', very white, and thus, very right.

Then it hit me like a fist to the face, like it always does, yet everytime startles me like the first time. Here I was again, at that place, that oh-so-familiar, but still shocking place that every person of colour visits at some point in their life, that irritating, nagging, itchy uncomfortable place that forces you to look at the mirror of contemplation and reflect on your reality—Yes, that confusing ill-feeling produced by the unconscious question: "Did this incident occur because the driver is just an anal-retentive, or did this occur because he is, once again, offended by her blackness?" The information is not blatant, he didn't call her a nigger, but deep down in the pit of your bowel, you know you've been mistreated, short-changed, disregarded, disrespected, devalued, abused or harassed simply because of your aggravating colour. And unlike White people, you are forced to wonder how often this occurs, when it may arise, and how it will negatively affect your life.
A hindrance. A worry. An irritating burden.

An irritated glance, does not mean someone dislikes the colour you are wearing, it means they dislike your colour. A prolonged stare in a convenience store does not mean they wish to know how they can be of service to you, it means they despise and mistrust you because you look like an obvious criminal (thanks to the media). Being pulled to the side of the road by police, when you're not speeding, is not an indication that the officer is simply inquiring as to your well-being, because his job is to serve and protect, it means that he, too, despises and mistrusts you and is looking for another dark inferior to dump his supremacist rage on. When they consistently clear their throats, as they read your application, it does not mean your qualifications have made them so excited they are choking on the words "You're hired!", it means they think your dreads have lice, your dialect is an English of the broken kind, you bathe in curry powder, you must be illiterate or at least stupid, you will use your power position to infest their cooperation with your kind, or at least seek racial revenge, you couldn't possibly be serious, and therefore are not quite white, I mean right, for the job. And when your 500-year-old W.A.S.P. Mass Media professor pauses when you raise the point that the Canadian education curriculum ignores the perspectives of people of colour, leaving us to turn to the media which then reinforces racial stereotypes, it does not mean that he is pausing so as to fully absorb and reflect on the valuable insight of a student he so admires, it means he is humouring you because he thinks you're just another angry Black person.

Now sometimes, that professor may actually be considering what you're saying, that officer may sincerely be concerned, that counter clerk truly dedicated to customer service, that potential employer truly considering you for the job, but unfortunately, you cannot automatically assume this. Instead, you must carry the burden of colour, ride the rollercoaster of paranoia, walk the walk of a marked person, be cautious of what you wear, what you say, and who you associate with. You and Jekyll and Hyde are brethren, you speak in various tongues and wear many masks, you always watch your back, in fear that your double life—your two-faced reality—will be exposed. You wake up in the morning and wonder how your colour is going to affect you that day. For the 'student', her colour, sex, age, class and style of dress made her particularly delicious prey. And while you deal with this submerged turmoil of 'everyday life', you must also combat all the forces that pressure you to internalize society's distaste of you, all the vices that divide and subdivide, all the pressures that make you resent others like yourself.

I board the next bus and my thoughts are interrupted by the young black man's voice next to me. "Yes, she showed us her card...it was her, and she had showed the driver twice already and he was still bugging her." "Well," replied one of the White men, "I think you're right. He wouldn't have bugged her that way if she was white. But these guys are under a lot of stress, you know...and sometimes they get like that…("Like what?" I thought… "Like racist?"). "Me and Jim are going to *Speakers' Corner* to complain." (How noble.) Even these White men who had been sitting at the back of the bus, during the incident, could smell the rotten sweaty stench under an unbathed, but perfumed body of racist evidence. The young Black man replied to my question about what occurred after I left: that the student did go back a third time to show her card, and the driver confiscated it, and she was left alone on the bus to deal with the scrutiny, disbelief, and potential harm and loss that were to be delivered by the police.

Immediately, I felt the sting of thousands of red ants carrying shame diligently up my back. How quickly I, and my 'coloured' people, had turned accusingly on the 'student'. Instead of addressing the 'driver', who physically controlled the movement of the bus, we blamed the student for stopping the bus, as if she actually could have. Instead of questioning the older, White male driver as to his justification for such hassle, we scrutinized the young, Black female victim of such harassment, assigning her blame for our inconvenience. And our 'embarrassed', 'coloured' West Indian speaker vocalized the slave mentality common to his generation, the helpless, powerless confession in the face of unjustified white supremist mistreatment. And our young, hip-hoppish black self-appointed attorney attempted to defend our dignity, personify our desired courage.

 I swallowed a lump of hopelessness caught in my throat. It was 1995— we didn't live in the 'violently racist Southern States'—we lived in the all-loving Canada. We no longer lived by segregation enforced by the code of the invisible colour line, no, we all got along; Rosa Parks was a historic symbol of resistance necessary for the past, but today I met a modern day Rosa Parks, a young poor Black woman who was not going to leave her seat on the bus, not because of the injustice of the 'Whites Only' policy, but because of the knowledge that her unjust harassment was triggered by a 'Whites Only' mentality. Same shit, different year.

 I realize this incident can in no way be compared to 400 years of slavery, rape of individuals as well as nations, genocide of aboriginal peoples around the world, modern day South Africa, historic lynching and torture of Blacks in the Southern States, police brutality in North and South America, and many other gross atrocities suffered by people of colour worldwide. But, I truly believe that incidents such as these facilitate more severe abuse of one's human rights as well as compound the psychological brutality against one's racial self-image and dignity. Who knows what happened when the police arrived? Based on past incidents in Toronto, we are aware that it is not impossible that our student could have been illegally and unjustifiably strip-searched and humiliated, solely because she was black, poor, and female, or shot in 'the back' for resisting arrest and concealing an invisible, I mean non-existent, weapon that was obviously a threat to the life of the armed officers involved. She, the student, was at the mercy of the White authority, which could rape, beat, interrogate, shoot, arrest, confine, humiliate, or manipulate her life as they pleased with no justification or repercussion from the Canadian Court or the Canadian people. So, while the student only lost her right to a TTC card, her self-esteem, time, safety, and respect, the point is that racist incidents like this are often the catalyst to severely unjust and brutally violent attacks on marked persons to which they have no defense or recourse.

And why? Because the marked, in this case, a young working-class Black female student, is guilty by association, association with the deviant, inferior, different element of society that threatens the homogeneity of the dominant class. She, being involuntarily associated to the powerless class must be kept at bay, must be kept divided, alone and marginalized, lest her and others like her resist the powers that be and threaten the whole hierarchical power structure the society is based on and the inequality it requires to maintain those in power, namely White, middle-class, able-bodied, heterosexual males. Thus, stopping a busload of poor people of colour (most likely on their way to work for White employers) to triple-check the I.D. of a young, poor Black girl, with the help of police, was not a 'normal' procedure of transportation, but rather a power statement, a method of making an example of a rebel, a method of instilling fear in the powerless, a mental submission and humiliation intended to reinforce and clarify the social power positions of both parties.

Yesterday, in the Southern States, I.D. was required to be in White areas. Today, in various parts of the world, I.D. is requested to be on the street after dark. Yesterday, I.D. was required at any time in South Africa. Today, I.D. is required at any time in South Africa. Yesterday, in the U.S., I.D. was required as proof of being a 'free man'. Today I.D. is required as proof of being a student at a high school or University. Yesterday, I.D. was required as proof of slave ownership. Today, I.D. is required as proof of being a legitimate human permitted to drive a nice car or as proof of a legitimate human permitted to ride the Rocket. Same shit, different year. Why do people of colour have to constantly identify themselves? Constantly have to defend their blackness? Who are they mistaking us for? Hmm. UP FROM SLAVERY! YES! FREE FROM SEGREGATION! YES! BUT BOUND BY DISCRIMINATION, BURNED BY DAILY PSYCHOLOGICAL HARASSMENT!

What we are dealing with today is not the brutal obvious mutilation of human beings based on race, but the residue of historic segregation, an undercover 'us and them' double standard code of conduct, and a repressed hypocritical policing of thought and liberty, of the powerless and marginalized. And our Canadian society has adopted this ideological domination, and abided 'peacefully' under its racist, patriarchal hegemony, this domination without use of physical force, just as the common-sense principle, that social location, policies, power structure and unjust treatment of individuals in a 'natural' code of conduct. For this ideological domination to function, it requires the majority of society (the masses), to believe in the integrity of its institutions, fear of its laws, and depend on its hegemony for moral direction.

Therefore if Blacks commit the most crime, as media depicts, then it is natural that there is a disproportionately large number of young Black males in prisons in North America. Therefore, if police are there to serve and protect, then no officer would carelessly shoot an individual because he thought of them as somehow expendable and invaluable as a human being, but rather his life would most definitely have had to have been in danger. In high schools of predominantly Black, Indian and Chinese students, the majority of teachers are White, simply because there are no qualified teachers of colour. Brandon Walsh of *Beverly Hills 90210* could date every girl he encounters, except his beautiful Black next door neighbour, because she had a boyfriend, naturally an uneducated Black cook living in the ghetto. But that's understandable. That's natural. That's common sense.

And women, people of colour, the working class and other marginalized and disadvantaged people also fall prey to this common sense principle. Unfortunately, this common sense principle often alienates us, separates us, disadvantages us, sabotages us, and wears and tears at our self-esteem, promoting fear and passivity in the face of authority, victim-blame and compliance to unjust acts, or at least silence in the face of them. Despite race, class, age, gender, etc., we often unknowingly ride a discriminatory school bus to a racist, homophobic, capitalist, and patriarchal school of thought. Driving our school bus is the privileged White male heterosexual, able-bodied, middle-class schoolmaster, who directs the bus, controls our thoughts, and instructs us on how to behave. Us, school children (dependent, powerless, inferiors) depend on his direction, his power to get us ahead, to move the bus along to a higher destination that he controls. We never question his authority, and we scrutinize, alienate, and separate from ourselves those who do. But what we don't realize is the schoolmaster is not only a 'master' of himself, but of those he considers inferior as well. And when someone defies his power, he cannot only stop the bus, make an example of the 'uppity' lesser (with reinforcement of armed troops), but can leave the rest of us destitute.

"Just show him the card." Just submit to his racist will. "Just show him the card." Just sacrifice your dignity so the bus will move. We depend on the bus to function in this society. Question the authority and we are all stranded— and we all want to get ahead. "Just show him the card." And if you don't we won't support you, we will leave you to face the troops alone, not because we want to, but because we are so down-trodden and we want to get ahead, we want the bus to move, and besides we are as targeted, helpless and powerless as you—so better "just show the card." Compliance. Question nothing and politely ignore injustice. Ride the Rocket. And get taken for a ride. That day, when I arrived at the school of thought, I had missed my class.

Just In Case You Wanted To Know:

After the racist bus incident, I felt concerned as to what happened to our young Black student. For four continuous days I tried to contact TTC Customer Services, only to be disappointed by a busy tone, answering machine or redirection. I also contacted the local Police Department (42 Division) and was told flatl, by the officer in charge that he "was not prepared to," (or would not) "answer that sort of question." When I asked him, in general, what was the nature and occurrence of racial incidents in the area. I was told by another officer that they would not give out any information regarding this incident, and that I would have to contact the TTC. I then contacted the *Toronto Star* and suggested this story, to which the person in charge stated, "If we don't call you back within a day, it means we aren't running the story." Well, my woman must have had cramped fingers 'cause my phone has yet to ring. But, of course, 'common sense' would tell you that these behaviours couldn't possibly be an avoidance, a denial, or means of silencing those marked persons of our liberal, 'kinder' nation.

the man who called me NIGGER

He was old and white.
The man who called me nigger.
He was short and fat.
The man who called me nigger.
He was stinky and dirty.
The man who called me nigger.
The man who called me nigger.
Who is the man that called me nigger?
He speaks incoherently.
Maybe he's a high school drop out;
or perhaps a bum;
or maybe he's a son.
A husband.
A father.
A grandfather.
He is old.
I should respect my elders.
He is a person.
I should love all people.
But tell me how I should feel about
The man who called me nigger.

sherrie outten

drum beats

If I close my eyes and listen
I hear it, faintly, still calling
the everlasting drum beat of my ancestry
calling me to retrace my past
to unite with my people and know the truth.

Above that distant beat,
I hear another still closer
the distinguishable sound of the steel drum
Its tempo increasing as I learn
of my birthplace and its roots.

Over top, another beat is growing
blending those of the past and present
using its knowledge of the past
to survive in the future
bringing the times closer together.

Each individual beat with its unique sound
is blended together with the rest
to try to unite its long lost people
by informing us of the truth
perhaps one day we'll all be 1.

asha noel

PatRiarcHy

On his demand, she consented

he moaned
she screamed
his grin
her grimace
eyes closed
hers open
lips parted
hers parched

relaxation rewarded, rigid frigidity
his sweat
her tears
his river
her rain

satisfaction
sacrifice

carol higgins

the aRt of POSSESSION
Strange Relationship

He had silky hair he used to touch when he talked to me. I was more aware of my looks when I looked at him. I didn't feel good enough in his light. Covered up imperfections until I was covering up bruises.

I met him at a mall in his cool clothes and with his smooth lyrics he convinced me that he was the one for me. I believed and fell into the trap that he set. My outer layers were eventually cut off and in my flesh were big hunkering bites.

Some looked disapprovingly as if that would make a difference. And some almost stopped and some tried to ask if I was alright. But he shooed them away with his slick talk. The same talk he used to reel me in. Words seemed to slide off his tongue, words seemed to wrap around my throat. And I was almost more afraid of his tongue and words than I was of his hands, his fists.

Contradicting hands used to hold me, caress me; same hands used to grip me and then beat me. He took my breath away with his looks; his punches. He made me

mansa

laugh with his jokes 'til I cried from his kicks. And then he bore into me with his dick.

His dick felt much like his eyes with which he tore into my soul; it turned to brittle bone—I still have the cracks to prove it. And yet my hips welcomed him. The more I loved him the more he owned me.

My legs, my breasts, my body was his. And I felt like a slate that he could create on. That he could design and manufacture. That he could put out for the world to see.

And sometimes it wasn't so blatant. And sometimes it wasn't out in the open. He would use communication like a knife. He would slice into me with his silence and then would pick up the pieces of me with new words of affection, of love.

Love was his game which he mastered like a pro and I played by the rules. He changed them at the drop of a hat. They governed the way I looked, the way I dressed, even the colour of toenail polish I wore. And I followed them to please him. I followed them for his approval.

I tell you that before you ask. I tell you that 'cause people ask the questions. The same people who stopped. They ask questions in their comfy offices, from their comfy lives. And I have simple answers that they seem not to understand. But nothing could be more simple than love.

And I sit here with his baby swimming in my belly and him miles away with his new catch. And I hope that it will not be a boy 'cause I would surely die if I had to raise another him. I sit with his baby swimming in my belly and I hope that it will not be a girl 'cause I wouldn't want to raise another me.

memory-bank MOVIES

by suzanne anderson

She remembers towering mango trees
banana trees
big red apple trees
pear-shaped
with white, tissue-like flesh
under the red skin
she remembers its sweet juice
running down the corners of her mouth

she remembers old hands
brown, veined hands
dragging a comb
through her thick hair
abundant with kinky-curls
she would cry
or not
depending on how elaborate a hair-style
those hands intended to create
and how long
the ordeal lasted

she remembers her blue skirt
and white blouse
the primary school uniform
she remembers envying the older girls
their uniform
identical to hers
but longer, with strange bumps
and curves

she remembers school
the Jamaican national anthem
ringing loud and proud
throughout the morning air
a prayer is said to complete
that morning's assembly

filing into the classroom
each of them avoiding the kids
with the dreadlocks
in their hair

(they all have lice
everyone knows that)

the kids with the dreadlocks
were dirty and poor
        the others were poor too
        but none of them knew
        the ones who did
        kept silent

see dick
see dick run
run dick run

she remembers not finding it strange
to see a white boy
run across the page
of the book
held by her Black hands

someone beside her gets the strap
they were late
or spoke out
or were too poor to buy the book
they all read from

no one looks
it's not polite to stare

she remembers another time
another class
many Black legs
crossed at the knees
they are sitting on the floor
for some reason
she notices the usual pairs of feet
dirty and hard
from their days of no shoes

on this day
she could see her feet too
she had taken off her shoes
on the way to school
she felt courageous, bold
and dirty

dirty,
not from the dirt
her feet had encountered
(on the way to school)
but from someplace in her mind
where she had never been

from someplace under her skirt
where no one had ever touched
save herself
and her grandma
who gave this place
(her secret place)
per functionary wipes
during baths

no one else touched her secret place
until this boy
who sat beside her
he was barefoot too
she remembers not liking the smell

she remembers a very tall
light-skinned boy
a friend of her uncle's
he wants her to sit on his lap
he has long skinny legs
and a really big thing
protruding through the hole
in his pants

she remembers not liking the smell

she remembers playing
in her new room
in her new home
in a new country
the memory-bank movie
of a little girl
sitting on top of a tall boy
the smell of his penis

she remembers dismissing this memory
she couldn't identify with the girl
in the movie
besides, there was no sound
and she wasn't yet old enough
to understand silent films

ROOM 9K

ayoola silvera

i don't have many memories of Grade 2, only clicks of scenes, like photographs but not so distant. Feelings in memory are hard to describe, but I'll try as best I can when I write about the one memory of Grade 2 that truly stands out from the others.

It was summertime, at recess, and my friends were on the swing. It was one of those swings that fit 3 people but we were small so we could squeeze on 5. I only asked if I could join them and to this day I have never understood their shocking reaction.

"Black cat! Black cat!" They were suddenly chanting words at me. "Black cat, Black sheep" anything black was me. I stood there until an older friend of mine (who was 10 or 11) came by and I asked him to help me. I didn't know what I wanted to be saved from; I only knew that they were hurting me. His response was an embarrassed shake of his head and a quick step away. Suddenly I felt so alone and cold all over in the hot summer sun. It seemed that everyone in the yard was yelling at me, "Black cat! Black sheep!" I didn't know what to do. I just stood there and cried.

Click. Then the memory takes a picture and that recollection ends. I only remember days later speaking with the principal, my mother strong beside me, and that was my last year at that school. It was years later that I realized that I was perhaps the only Black student attending that school, but I never experienced an incident of racism that froze in my mind like that. I've always wondered why.

DISmissed...

natasha gomez-bonner

dismissed
You have been
Dismissed
No longer needed
No longer wanted
You serve no purpose
Dismissed

Crying?
What are you crying for?
You knew the score
the deal
the 411

Puppy eyes won't save you
Just put yourself together
Get out
Hey Baby!
It's that sim...

Note: She Blew him away.
To her, it had to stop somewhere.

the pussy is Ours

another Black woman perusing the issue of heterosexual interracial relationship

I was talking to a Black woman about a weekly event when she expressed a desire to have a good venue to fully appreciate rap and hip hop; she brusquely cut me off with "…I'm not interested in going there. There are no Black men!" Now I know this event is practically 50/50 Black men, and men of no colour (This term is a response to the phrase "of colour" used to identify and refer to African, Asian, and all indigenous peoples). And none of these Black men, severe in their strong presence and proudly shaking trembling dreadlocks as a direct tool of Blackness, have a Black woman partner: Even the "*hair-liberated* and therefore *politically conscious of Blackness*" Black men prefer the "*lighter the better*" fad; why should both the "*hair-liberated*" and "*hair-enslaved*" Black women persistently see it as their birth responsibility to save the race? It becomes an issue for consideration when quite a few Black women are happy to affirm their status as the property of Black men and therefore must consistently validate this by showing their rigid resolution to date **Black men only**. The Black woman seems to have forgotten that Africa holds the most genetically diverse race of people. The vast sprawling West Africa, which is supposedly the birthplace of the "Negro", is a home of heterogeneity and diversity both in physical attributes and cultural aesthetics. A neocolonial Black man cannot sympathize with the racial and sexual oppression a Black woman has to put up with on a day-to-day basis any better than a man of no colour.

Black women continue to see themselves as the strong amazonic provider of racial continuity to Black men and the Black race in North America. However, this burden of racial responsibility is never a matter of concern for Black men. The ingrained colonial desire to possess the "fair lady" has always been understood as an indication of status and whiteworld mainstream acceptance by Black men, not only in the diaspora, but also in the continent.

II
the continent's intolerance in this context

Growing up in Nigeria, I recall a much relished argument amongst student friends about who was more colonized: the Nigerian man or the Nigerian woman. Though the question here is not mere comparison, it is essential to note that Black men in the continent had more contact with the colonial masters than Black women, who were heavily protected by the men and by the society at large, for fear of contamination through sexually transmitted colonial disease. And so, while the African woman still adhered to and supported the traditions of the society, the African clerk, fastidiously serving the colonial governor and vigorously protecting his own wife, began to envy the White man his White woman; most especially since he was in an opportune position to travel to the racist whiteworld where the White woman had been released from her pre-slavery and colonial era status to a position which was undoubtedly above the Black man and, consequently, the Black woman.

In patriarchal African cultures, to possess "another man's woman" is to have equal social status with that man, to be level with him or elevated above him. In West Africa, the whiteworld is perceived as immoral and promiscuous in relation to sex and marriage. And as a result of both the patriarchy existing in West Africa and the African man's knowledge of the White woman's exotification of him as a sexually capable virile male, the White woman is particularly perceived as de-culturalized and sexually immoral. The African man possessing a White woman is accepted, since it is believed men have little to lose from sexual knowledge of these women or any woman at all. However, for an African woman to desire or engage in a similar relationship with a (sexually loose) White man is socially despicable. She becomes the shameless, contaminated creature who must be ostracized by the community and remain unmarried to an African man. It makes little difference whether or not she is/was married to her White partner. The stigma she bears is forever reaffirmed by the presence of any material wealth she may possess, which is seen as gifts from her colonial fornicator. (In most patriarchal African cultures, women are not allowed to own property.)

It is often argued in my native West Africa that the African man with the White woman/wife is not an issue of neocolonialism, as it is generally understood that these men, and society at large, will never consider such a relationship as binding, since it holds none of the cultural respect and traditions encompassing a similar relationship with an African *blood daughter*. (Even though at the time of such a relationship with a White woman, these men disassociate themselves from their community and display internalized colonial pompous "been to" attitudes towards their own people.) Often such men will later seek to be "properly" married to a African woman. This later marriage completely nulls the previous relationship with the White woman. There are quite a few African mixed-race children from such circumstances. As long as these children have African fathers, they are accepted as legitimately African, since there is no such thing as an illegitimate child when the father is African. Should the maternal parentage be African while the paternal is not, the rule is completely reversed. And so, while the African man may bring back a White woman as wife or co-parent, the African woman is forbidden to engage in any form of relationship—platonic or otherwise—with the

White man in her African country for fear of severe isolation, ridicule, and disrespect.

While this may have been a good protection against the racist White man's ideology of the exotic, inertly animal sexual Black woman, it has done little to eliminate the global stereotyping and objectification of the Black woman's sexuality, particularly of certain so-called typically West African female body parts. It has done little to eliminate the racism and sexism of the whiteworld against the Black woman, or the unapologetic sexism of the Black man against the Black woman, both in the continent and diaspora.

III
was the Black man ever emasculated?

The fact that the Black woman continues to feel compelled to soothe and satisfy the Black man's needs so that she will not be seen as rejecting the Black community—while the Black man continues to defend his biased racial preference as the re-maculation of his status as a man and as the result of his inability to get along with Black women (he immediately puts the blame on Black women)—is a grave indication of the sad sexist and white-washed minds we live in. Quite a few Black women feel their loyalty is to Black men (as opposed to self) for reasons of racial identity, and because of the racist oppression experienced by these men. In doing this, we further promote a distorted history, which consistently maintains that the Black woman has but negligible scars from racist horrors mostly experienced by Black men, and that man suffering is a more dire situation than woman suffering. Due to the oppressive sexual disparities existing in the modern age, Black men's experience of racial guilt is easily ridden by their complaint of the de-masculation of their manhood through racism, and their assertion that they now deserve to possess the White man's prize. As much as I am aware that racism has taken its toll on Black men, I find it profoundly sexist that these same men instill acute pressure of racial guilt and intolerance towards the Black woman in similar situations. Black men continue to promote and reinforce the White racist glorification of the woman of no colour as the ultimate feminine prize. It is interesting to observe that the idea of Black women assuming a similar position and objectifying the White man as the ultimate masculine prize has apparently not occurred to Black men. This is because Black men have **never** lost their sexist masculine status. They have felt comfortable in a sexist and racist system where the image of the Black man is used to represent the Black race, and the White woman is the sole symbol of the female gender.

IV
lesbian racial betrayal?

In the gay 90s, quite a few Black women are openly defining their political identity not only as Black women advocating feminism, but also as lesbians. It is interesting to note that while one may find more lesbian Black women involved with lesbian White women, this is not always seen by the heterosexual Black male sub-community as racial betrayal. Due to the sexist patriarchal system existing today, a Black woman in an interracial relationship with a white would be regarded by the Black man, not as betraying the race but as betraying (Black) men. However, a Black woman advocating feminism and active resistance to sexism (and its inter-relatedness with racism) would be more likely to be perceived as betraying the race. This is because Black people believe feminism to be a White woman's concept. American White feminists, in their efforts to perpetuate White supremacy, have consistently denied the ancient and modern-day resistance of the African woman (both in the continent and diaspora) and woman of colour against male domination in their communities, and their contribution in empowering masses of women in similar situations of economic and sexist oppression.

Another point to consider is the fact that men in general do not equate lesbianism with the threat of male homosexuality. After all, considering the status of womanhood (even with the so-called emancipation of [White] women through North American [White] feminist ideology, and the sheer economic necessity of changes in sex roles in other cultures), two women openly loving each other is more or less two powerless persons loving freely.

As a heterosexual Black woman advocating feminism, as much as I may have wished for the ability to respond to a woman sexually due to my political affiliation with feminism, I still question the sentiment that feminism should be defined as lesbianism. For Black women advocating feminism, and dealing with the day-to-day struggle to end the racism of the whiteworld, the sexism of racist White men as it is particularly experienced by Black women and women of colour, and the misogynist sexism of Black men, it may become necessary to seek immediate transformation through the avoidance of contact with men, and/or celibacy. It is important to make the point that as radical feminism is increasingly defined by lesbianism, heterosexual feminist Black women are made to feel like lukewarm outsiders.

V

Due to the stark reality of racism, sexism and class struggle which we are faced with as Black women, we may find it ridiculous for a Black woman to be involved in a permanent relationship with a man of no colour. The tools for support appear to be lacking in such relationships. The perceived sole reason for such an involvement remains the same reason that has been imposed on the psyche of the Black women everywhere by a racist sexist patriarchal system. In believing this, we use the same reasoning that lies behind the sexist claims against (Black women's) interracial relationships, with roots imbedded in the Black man's image of us as property in a racist and colonialist world. As Black women, when we criticize another Black woman because of the race of her partner, we merely jump onto the bandwagon of sexism prevalent in the community, regardless of our outwardly political stance in the resistance of racist and sexist oppression.

While I do advocate unity between Black women and men, I feel that as a people who have come this far in dealing with the reality of racial terrorism, we shouldn't be afraid that the challenges inherent in the transformation of problems within the community will divert our focus from the struggle to end racism. Without denying the fact that there are Black men, both in the continent and diaspora, who are supportive of Black women's liberation from racist and sexist oppression, I feel the need to challenge the sexist attitudes of Black men on two points. Firstly, I believe that failure of Black men in the diaspora to critically challenge that perverse characteristic of an oppressed group has created a fertile ground for the Black community's divisive self-hate to be displayed through blatant misogyny. Black men have recently begun to approach and challenge their self-hate, but this has been mainly directed towards (the media instituted and instigated concept of) *Black men on Black men*.

And secondly, I want to challenge the ways Black men in general view Black women as property, whose move towards self-liberation (either through feminist politics, or sexually/racially different partners), is seen as undermining and threatening their status as men. Just as Black women do not own Black men, Black men do not own Black women. There has been and will continue to be racial mixing. Suppressing one group for sexist reasons creates a false sense of unity.

VI

Having personally known African women in the continent who have gone through estrangement from their community due to their relationship/marriage to men other than African men, and having also known African men whose status has been neocolonially elevated when they have brought home the decorative white feather, I feel the need to speak for these women's silence. And to those Black women who refuse to challenge their own rigid insistence that identification with Blackness and Black Struggle can only come through relationships and sexual allegiance to Black men: **our pussy belongs to us.**

Brothas

Brothers say sistas don't seem to understand
the plight of the oppressed broken Black man
They say that our eyes don't clearly see
Their pain! Their hurt! and Their tragedy

Brothers insist that we can't relate
They've been o-ppressed, dis-tressed, and so-pressed by fate
and then there are brothers who come strong and correct
Speaking of Nubian Princesses and eternal respect
But when push comes to shove those brothers all switch
And you become D-moted, D-graded to an African bitch
Brothers feel that if the truth is bad we must hide
suffer in silence and relinquish our pride
Hold our heads high and keep our backs strong
Fight in their army as though nothing were wrong

Brothers have convinced us that affection is a game
That **Baby** and **Mother** should be our first and last name
That holding hands and hugging are simply all white
But those same brothers get oh so affectionate at nights

Brothers say…
That I should have nothing to say
Keep smiling and hoping for a brighter new day
But brother there's something you must understand
I will live with…
Not die for the African man `

jay pitter

rewind my SELECTA!

moist bodies groovin to dih dance hall beat
dih pawty did pack up pon Franklin Street
man a do dih peppaseed, crush smaddy new boot
two yout locked in a game of trivial pursuit

Im did shoot to kill
an im no shoot an miss
what a contravesy is dis
tongues void of negotiation
false machismo demands termination
staccato of bullets puntuate dih soun
perferated corpse soaks dih groun
select dance hall vibe promote dis murda
dooh rude bwoy, nuh tek it no furda
Buyaka! Buyaka! Annadah one gawn
Kumbaya mih Lawd, Kumbaya
Rewind my Selecta,
Rewind antil yuh find
Redemption Song!

"Pssssssssss!
Hey sexy gal, wha yuh ah seh?"
bulging eyes strip mih form as if to devowa
mih jus cut me two y'eye an look pon im sowa
when im realize seh im nah get no play
hear wha dih outta awda, limp foot, sequin, gold teet
bwoy tell mih seh!

karen lee

Im love im brownin an me is too blackenin
hair waan Vidal Sassoon, face fi eva baboon!
rejecting cocoa, chocolate an rich earth hues
lowing whitebread ideals fih im fih choose
skin tones fair, sand, snow, mix or bleached
brainwash by colour politics of deceit
divisive legacy recycle tru time
Rewind my Selecta
Rewind antil yuh find
Redemption Song!

Ee-hee! Yuh fuck six gals las nite an it was sweet?
Maxine, Charmaine, Jackie, Paulette, Trix
an dih one named Margeurite?
im nuh use notten name latex
dis ya idiot bwoy get mih spirit vex
im seh im did possess wid dih glimmity, glammity
ignorant of consequent genital calamity.

2.

What a dreadful condition in Babylon
yuh same one a bawl disease deh bout sake a battyman
when a yuh, yuh is dih donagon
yuh love boas seh yuh no powda man
but yuh a sprinkle we wid dih possibility of HIV
AIDS a go roun an we nuh waan catch it
Rewind my Selecta,
Rewind antil yuh find
Redemption Song!

Now im get vex an threaten me
wid one bloodclaat, what not, which not, rassclaat
tomp inna my big ead!

My ead? My crown?
Age old truths housed in me temple
violated at dih hands of an illiterate simple?
limited intellect caan effect communication
tru physical violence lies my devaluation
women prey to the tyranny of misogyny
dih same predicament ahead fih owa progeny
fih box a ooman is not a crime but a duty?
Rewind my Selecta, Rewind
Abuse of ooman is a serious crime
Rewind my Selecta,
Rewind antil yuh find
Redemption Song!

Awo! Mih gwan on like my pussy line wid gold?
Rewind my se-lec-ta! Come Again!
Yuh nuh gwine stab it up, jack it up, dig out my meat
cah my vagina line wid gold
an fit fih a King wid tongue as spoon to eat!
so yuh betta jus mind
cah yuh know seh yuh caan dine
restricted from my fruit sublime
Rewind my Selecta,
Rewind antil yuh find
Redemption Song.

Abandon ooman's historic objectification
challenge simultaneous penis glorification
from ooman's loins men became
tru perverse sexual politics dih phallus reigns?
compounded in a male universal mind
reiterated in select dance hall vibe
Rewind my Selecta,
Rewind antil yuh find
Redemption Song!

3.

Negate warped colour politics of deceit
which reject woolly hair, dark skin an full lips
Redeem bullet-stricken bloodspills
of pawns in yuh wicked game of "shoot to kill"
severed penis of battybwoy stuffed in their mouths
promiscous, heterosexual penis, unsheathed, aroused
swollen, throbbing vaginas, clitoris denied
rape commanded by misogynist dance hall vibe
female heads bounce awff yuh angered fists
skin torn by dih switch to dih beat
"Kill dih bitch"!?!
Rewind my Selecta,
Rewind antil yuh find
Redemption Song!

Name dat tune,
lyrics echoed by many voices gawn before
riddims which unite, inspire, uplift, restore
answer to dih call of the monster drum…beats
mesmerize, ipnotize, mobilize
dih now colonized mind
Rewind my Selecta, Rewind
quench famine in dih desert of your enslaved mind
awaiting liberation
from select dance hall indoctrination
Disgraceful Abomination
in a pressed an trying time

Rewind my Selecta, Rewind
Rewind my Selecta, Rewind
Rewind my Selecta, Rewind
antil yu find
Redemption Song!

United we stand Departed we FALL

20 minutes later, BANG, the shots rang out loud,
People stared, screaming, chaos was in the crowd.
Shot three times in the back, no significant reason at all,
We have to remember, united we stand, departed we fall.

My friend's brother was stabbed in the back,
Ten stitches he got, what a brutal attack.
Jumped into a fight, got deeply involved,
We have to remember, united we stand, departed we fall.

A sixteen year old boy got stabbed in the chest,
Blood sprayed everywhere, a witness confessed.
Now he is gone forever due to a fight I recall,
We have to remember, united we stand, departed we fall.

Slashed across his face with a Swiss army knife,
A fight over territory on a horrid cursed night.
Another brother down how can we stand tall,
We have to remember, united we stand, departed we fall.

Why do the brothers keep killing each other,
Everyday in the news or on the front cover.
We have to hear the message, a community call,
That United We Stand, Departed We Fall.

ngardy contch

you said you loved me and i was your woman

You said you loved me,
and I was your woman.
So one day you laid me
down on the bed
and deeply and carefully
cut out
a triangle
from between my legs.

You said that you loved me,
and I was your woman.
So you locked
the prism of flesh
in a shiny crystal glass case
and placed it
on your livingroom
mantle place,
for your friends
to see
and not touch, taste, or smell.

roxanne tracy

You said you loved me,
and I was your woman.
So you chained me
to the bed
and made me
watch you
as my now
rotting prism
pleasured you.

Time slowly ticking the day into night.

You said that you loved me,
and I was your woman.
So you came
crystal case in hand
and told me
you wanted
a family.
Locking the case tightly
when it was over.

You said that you loved me,
and I was your woman.
So when my belly swelled,
you buried
the prism
deep beneath the earth.

You said that you loved me,
and I was your woman.
So I have gone
in search of
my prism
to someday find
what love is…

Un-rest

monique wilson

Conflict within our troubled souls.
Forgotten are dreams, hopes and goals.
Guns are loaded. Now the violence begins.
But why are we fighting when no one can win?
Who are the victors? The men who survive?
Are they winners just because they're alive?
We are constantly fighting or arguing it seems,
Over different beliefs and different dreams.
Harmony and peace seem hard to obtain.
Will we ever tire of inflicting pain,
Upon each other? I wish we all could see,
How much peace would mean for someone like me.

un-titled

hands grope.
Combative fingers
   push away.
But the hands persist
   intruding
   invading
private territory.

My back is against the wall
as his face nears mine
The enemy is closing in.

His body is against me:
there is nowhere to run.
A battle ensues —
I lose.

The soft mattress
rises up beneath me
The softness
that should be so comforting
is instead a hindrance,
It yields too easily
to my unyielding form.

The gates to my private fortress
are wrenched open
as the intruder
storms the entrance

yvette francoso

Bile rises
as I try to fight off the enemy
But he refuses to retreat

Trapped,
energy waning,
I feebly launch
one last defence attack

It does not work.
My battle cry
becomes a whimper.

Tongue
and teeth
riddle me like grenades

His passion
becomes my pain.
Intimacy
becomes a battleground
for control

But his ammunition
is more powerful
than mine.

I raise the white flag.

Silently,
Reluctantly,
I admit defeat.

The last vision I see
before my soul dies
is of the tiny crucifix
dangling
from my captor's neck

Suspended
Just inches below
my enemy's once warm
    friendly
smile.

• •

don't touch it

*b*rother,
I know you want to find
my firm, tight round behind
that you seem to think is so fine,
but don't touch it.

yvette francesca

I know you ache to snare
my robust, full derriere
that proudly sticks up in the air,
but don't touch it.

You may just be mistaken,
thinking, "it's out there: it's for the takin'"
But that's not your decision to be makin'
So don't touch it.

Didn't you listen? Didn't you hear
when Granny used to box you 'cross your ear
and say, "That doesn't belong to you, dear—
don't touch it?"

Why then, now that you're grown
would you treat this as your own
and ignore my protests and my groans
to touch it?

Whether it's a leg, a butt, or a bust
You crave, take a picture if you must
But learn to control your carnal lust
and please don't touch it.

When i was Real

*h*ad I been a real woman
maybe I would have run
with open arms to you
Might have smiled while you called me
Sugar, baby, honey, schnookie even
Might have blushed when you told me
how tasty I looked
Ready for you to take a bite
But I couldn't bear the thought
of seeing myself on yet another menu

And so I was reduced to being called a bitch
A cop-out is what that is
To you every woman is a bitch
first 'cause she's out for the money
then 'cause she's out for the fame

mansa

Maybe just 'cause she's out
She's a woman
No explanation needed
Some kind of weak sex, fragile
Praised only when she has to act
more like a man
Rough and Ready
to somehow turn into a real woman
A high-heel wearing, stand by her man,
real woman
A real woman with false lashes and inches of makeup trying to hide the fact that she's
Desperate for your real man love
Paranoid someone else might get your superlatives
In all their splendour
An instant mommy to you and all the kids you'll "give" me
I'll "give" you
which is politically correct in "Real Woman Land"?
I would rather be a real woman working to pay more than just the daycare and diaper bills
doing more than just mothering you
I love you but I didn't carry you for nine months
and I'm not gonna carry you for the rest of my life
I love you but I don't seem real enough for you
With my arms wide open I would run to you
But I can't see through these lashes and
I'm afraid I might break a heel.

my ex

*h*e's in love with a girl
who has never been true
to the 2001 older men she's been through
Blood starts racing through his veins
for a girl who's done crack
she would lay on her back
to get money for that!
and she has
He get weak in the knees
for a girl who dropped school
so she could roam the streets
as if she is cool!
His heart skips a beat
for a girl who steals and don't care
so she can have fake nails, make-up,
and a weave in her hair
He day dreams of a girl
who's carrying another man's baby
It's crazy
but I'm happy for him
He's in love

kim outten

Recipe for a NEGRO

*f*irst, blend together the usual ingredients
found in everyone:

    2 eyes
    2 ears
    2 feet
    1 heart
    200 and something bones etc.
    Add plenty of tears
Then with care apply brown skin.

lisa hollingsworth

RAINBOW OF LOVE

charee metz

today I heard
The same old
Racist remarks
Why can't you understand
Words do hurt?

And you hide
Behind your mask
Afraid of me
Believing the colour
Of my skin
As lethal as a gun

But don't you hear
The children singing,
And they are singing,
"We're making
A rainbow of love
And there is
A pot of gold
at the end."

I saw them

Blacks and Whites
Different cultures
Holding hands
Loving each other
Yet, you
Blinded by
Your hatred
Refuse to see
The beauty in me

Hey, don't you
Think it's time
You and I
Got together
I offer you
My hand
Let's join in
This rainbow of love.

Oh, listen
Can't you hear
The children singing
"We're making
a rainbow of love
And there is
A pot of gold
At the end."

Hit of poison
Charee Metz

White powder
Up her nose,
Needles in her arms

Her world
So darn high
Shadows and hallucinations
No damn perceptions

Freebase or whatever
May be the case
She turns a few tricks
For a hit of poison

Hey girl,
You pretty one
Listen to the pulsation
Of your heart,
The fizz
Of your brain cells
And tell me,
Is this how you
You want it to be?

Dancing her psychotic
Drug induced dance
Little girl lost
Cries herself to sleep

Dance, dance dear child,
But why not dance
To dreams of tomorrow?

UNCONTROLLABLE feeling

i have an uncontrollable feeling inside
of me that I cannot control or stop.

wendy davis

It has a mind of its own that goes away with laughter
but it hits me hard with pain.

Sometimes I want it to take hold
of me, I want to die with it,
I am an addict.
I need to have more of it
just to make it through the day.
I get so angry and sad and angry,
so angry that I could kill anyone or anything,
but when I relax it goes away
until the next time…

the Body

One night I had the strangest dream
Of myself, beside a tree—
Blood laid fresh upon the root,
But on it had the strangest fruit—
Pale brown bodies hung by rope,
Swollen tongues—no final hope.
Within each eye, a story laid,
Of freedom songs and debts unpaid.
Just once I stopped and almost cried,
I saw a face I recognised.
The body stretched her hand to me,
And sang sweet songs of being free.
I held her hand until she died,
And through it all, she only smiled.
Then I saw the light of day,
Was dirty with a dingy grey.
But in the darkness of the night,
I heard a coffle gang in plight.
I hid my face and pursed my lips—
I heard the sounds of falling whips.
The black curtains had fallen down,
Within it held the painful sounds—
The clanking of the burden chains,
The bodies bawled out loud in pain.
The cooling air of the night breeze,
The bodies swayed among the trees.
And in the quiet of the strong,
The bodies sang their freedom songs.
Then someone tugged on my torn sleeve,
There stood a child, sad and bereaved.
"Why?" sad eyes seemed to say,
Unable to answer, I led her away.

jennifer holland

the Occurrence

paula avril french

*d*eliberate concentration let her see the dusky dawn. Suddenly there were only ten minutes before darkness would pervade the morning. The dawn came in quick grey, then pale light diffusing itself to lighten her room. She still was aware of the dark shadows around her, preventing the fullness of daylight.

It was necessary for her to concentrate on the coming morning, to focus on anything that would dispel her mental churning. But the thoughts came anyway. He did it./I know./He would never do that, she said./She looked me in the eye when she said it.

Her thoughts turned to the bed below her. Its thick, and plentiful, soft comfort delighted her, and she could feel sleep slowly returning, drugging her thoughts, scattering logic.

"Lou?" The sound of her mother's voice jolted her, bringing her close to tears. She knew her day had involuntarily begun. She moved slowly but evenly from the bed and began to dress. Her bedroom door opened.

"Didn't you hear me calling you?" Her mother stood partly in the doorway, one hand on the door frame, one on the doorknob, as if her leanness needed support.

Lou did not return her gaze. She knew her mother was not angry. It was not hard for her to read her mother; parading her every opinion was the woman's standard procedure. Ready or not, she brought it forth. It was usually something that produced a noticeable reaction: hot confrontation, shrinking submission, vibrating shock, puzzled fear. Lou knew few who could ignore her mother. Her variety of tongues—deadly accurate indirect insults, wit meant to shame but rarely to affirm, developed, animated gossip, sly hints or throat sounds wrapped in abuse, conversation concluders indicating ineptness, irresponsibility, weakness and especially displeasure, compliments for those few deemed worthy—was too ever-present, persistent, exact, loud, hitting the eardrums, again and again, demanding a need for some response. Indifference was rarely an option taken by listeners.

But change had come, something Lou instantly noticed and felt she could explain. Lou was sure it was her mother's decaying health that had gentled her bite, lowered her fire and intensified her humility, forcing her to re-examine every last thing and body she had ever come into contact with. Lou knew that she, too, came under this scrutiny; she was watched, analyzed. But what surprised her was her mother's re-examination of her as a possible ally, friend, comforter during the time when she would finally cease to breathe. She opened up to Lou, without warning or introduction, speaking as if compelled, using her new tone and approach to seek forgiveness for her past harshness. She told about her life, longings, pains and her few precious joys.

At first Lou felt prickly confusion and irritation when her mother spoke of herself and looked for sinister motives behind the offering of this information. But this evilness began to wear her down. So she turned to examine the knowledge. She began to see past the disease on her mother's face, see her mother as she must have been when she could envision no limits. A younger body saying such words and doing such passionate deeds. Wrinkles gone, fresh-faced, body flexible, life-slate clean. She wanted to see this woman-mother when she was single and full of expression, when she held tightly to dreams. Big dreams.

Lou glanced at the old body in her doorway. "Yes, I heard you. I was coming."

"Oh." Her mother watched her daughter get dressed in her usual jeans and burlap frock and allowed her eyes to leisurely wander around the room. "Well you could have answered or something," she said lightly, as if half preoccupied with something else. "I'll need your help today, if dinner is going to be ready by six o'clock." Her mother paused for a moment, breathing deeply. "And open a window or something."

Lou moved but deliberately did not address her mother's comment. She headed for the mirror and examined her chestnut face. She thought she might have gained weight.

"You're not taking a shower?" her mother asked.

Lou kept her eyes on the comb going through her temporarily thick afroed hair. "I had one, Mom. I just wanted to lie down for a few minutes." It was obvious to both of them that the words were strained, passing through clenched teeth. They exchanged quick looks and then, with a turn of dismissal, her mother said, "I want you to start with the bread. . ."

Lou walked behind her mother down the narrow hallway, listening with only as much consciousness as was necessary. She began to think of the quiet and independence of her own home, and the time she had been away from it since taking on the role of her mother's live-in nurse. She had loved its shelter. Remembering how she once dressed in silks, complete cottons, clothes that matched, how she had once had a full-time job she liked, how she had once had a life, she thought of the doctor's repeated phrase: It was only a matter of time now. She felt guilty knowing she could not wait for the time to expire. Her sense of confinement escalated as her thoughts returned to him. He did it/I know he did.

They entered the kitchen, and Lou smiled at the coming sunlight. It promised a warm day in the midst of winter's hold on the year. Its brightness did not as yet warm the small room, but Lou envisioned how the heat would come, how the sunlight would glide through the white, thin curtains, which were already pulled back so that as many rays as possible could come in. The streams of natural light would hit the white floor, counters and stove, and would cover the centred table.

Lou stood in front of the kitchen window, arms outstretched, eyes closed, head back, back arched, hoping for anything to come to her awareness and ease her pain. It was an almost histrionic pose and she could feel her mother standing behind her, watching her, expecting her to say something to explain the thrust of her body movement.

But she said nothing. Instead she opened her eyes and saw the familiar landscape that took her back too far into safe memories, memories that conflicted with what she now knew. It was too comfortable; too much analysis was needed for understanding. She turned away.

"Get those rolls going, Lou, you do them well. We need about twenty-four, so double the recipe."

"I know, Mom, I know," Lou responded flatly.

They worked in silence, Lou glancing sideways now and then to capture a glimpse of her mother's concentrating face. Her mother spoke suddenly, with softness: "I've been thinking about what you said." Lou watched as she stopped scrutinizing the beets and carrots before her, and after a while looked up. "I still think you're wrong. Mr. Combs wouldn't do that to you. To anyone."

"I know what he did, what I felt, Mom"

"He has a wife, for goodness. . ."

"So?"

"Maybe. . ." Her mother sighed. "I think you're confused."

Lou did not respond. Her anger, then resignation, then frustrated tears rose and she wished to let them overflow her. She was tired of justifying and explaining. The dull, draining pain that often invaded her temples made itself known.

"Anyway, all you young girls with a little prettiness get the wrong ideas," her mother said with a short laugh.

It was not so much the statement but the laughter that caused Lou to break her silence.

"Mom, I'm not stupid. The man touched me on my behind!"

"I know where. You said. I know."

"Then. . ." Lou bit her lip and closed her eyes so her mother wouldn't see them roll. "Look. Don't believe me if you don't want to, but telling me I'm wrong isn't going to make this go away." Her mother turned toward the sink to wash the vegetables, breaking into one of the long streams the sun was sending out. There was more to say, but Lou paused when she saw the look of grief her mother carried. She was not sure if it was for her or for Combs, or if it was a look of self-pity. She needed to know. She needed to clear her mind of voices, of the doubt re-analysis brought on. She wanted to clear her mind of shame.

"I just don't know why you're defending him, Mom. From the moment he moved into the neighbourhood years ago, I and all the kids knew he was strange."

Lou felt that the reasoning was immature, but she did not care. She also knew it to be untrue. Only her best friend Gladys disliked Combs: Gladys liked no one initially. Lou remembered the first time she saw him. He was so polite, a kind man with a kind wife. Cheerful, friendly, interesting, he bought the neighbourhood children huge candy canes at Christmas, told them stories that made sense, raced with them down the hill spanning the back of the townhouse complex her parents lived in. Women liked him. He went to church, listened to his wife in public, never cussed his wife in public, mowed his lawn and grew flowers that he courteously handed to all the females he could find. Men liked him. He was not only a good carpenter and all-around handy man, helping with broken down this and thats, but he had a firm understanding of the dealings of men and with money and public and private laws. He was not to be distrusted; his actions confirmed this for everyone. Even Gladys eventually came around.

"He just likes to play, Lou."

"This is no play thing, Mom. He's done it more than once." The confirmation in her voice was as much there to reassure herself of his actions as to convince her mother.

It came quick. "Well I just hope you don't get no stupid ideas in your head and go and make this public or something like that!"

Lou watched her mother and knew she was sorry for her words. She accepted her silent apology.

They worked mainly in silence for the rest of the day, verbally gaming occasionally. Noon came, and the food was prepared. They discussed Combs and his intentions, his reasoning, his life. By three o'clock, the dishes were washed, the walls checked for splatters of anything, the floors mopped and vacuumed. The smell of polish lingered. They discussed each other with less insult and pain than Lou thought would be present. The house stood ready for the subtle inspection of visitors; it was a fortress of clean.

"You should tell Dad, next time he wants to bring guests he should help." Lou said as lightly as she could.

"Ha. That'll be the day. You know they'd be eating out of cans if your father cooked."

"I guess you were right to start early." Lou leaned against the wall, looking out the kitchen window at the picked and winter-infertile garden in her parent's small plot of backyard. She could clearly remember Combs helping her mother start the garden, showing her how to tenderly nurture the vegetable in to growth. He had gently laughed at her mother's mistakes. Lou, then fourteen, had watched his bent back in the sun and trusted him completely, never once assuming he would ever touch her without his usual fatherly love. An acceptable touch.

"Better be prepared."

"So what now?" Lou turned to face her mother. She wanted to be sure to catch any offer, any word her mother said about Combs. She wanted to see all of her face, her intentions when she talked about him.

"Rest, just rest," was all her mother said.

Why now?/Didn't do this when I was in college./Now when I'm breaking twenty-five./Never all the times when I visited his house alone at 14, 15, 16, 11, 10./I just didn't notice?/Why now?/I wonder if he would do it to Gladys if she was here?/Last time I was doing him a favour./Helping him bring his groceries into his house./Him standing behind me./Putting his hand where it didn't belong./Does his wife know he's doing this?/Is he crazy?/Shocked, although he had done it before?/I step forward, and turn around./ His disgusting and revealing smile./Telling me, yes, he meant to do it./ He said it all through his smile./He could be my Daddy./But he did it.

Lou sighed to herself. "Go rest, Mom."

"Yeah, for an hour or so. Then I have to get up and look good for these people. I may be dying but. . ."

"You're not dead yet," Lou finished for her.

"Exactly."

Watching her mother's back struggle against weariness, Lou felt exhausted. She still had the voices within her to contend with and knew her life, their lives, would go on as usual; she knew they would stop for nothing or no one, never mind to address a series of recent, apparently simple touches and prolonged suggestive grins in the narrow hallway or kitchen, or living room of a man she had known practically her whole life. But the complexity of apparent simplicity was hers to deal with. He did it./I don't know why./But he did it.

He had slipped into her sphere of privacy uninvited when she did not think he ever would. He had hurt her, for she had trusted their relationship to cause him to behave differently. He had caused her confusion, for she could not imagine a reason, other than a perverted one, why a man she once thought of as beautiful would do this to her.

She knew that with time she would pass into a new awareness and strength, but she did not know where the newness would send her. She was too brain-worn to delve. And she was no longer sure whether her mother doubted her, or was simply too scared of the effects it would have to look right into the occurrence and understand it all.

She headed for the living room, with its view of the sunset. Nestled into a chair, she watched the shadows that already filled the corners of the room, as they began to edge out and completely take over the light, until darkness dominated. Then she would switch on the lights, and wait for her father to bring his guest home to a wel-washed house, to a table filled with food. They would eat, talk and be merry, with the evening sliding by into the stillness of night. And she would continue to see the smile of Combs and reach for her peace.

WE aRe FaMiLy

*d*ry cereal, no milk for days
mom will snap out of it
anytime they say; continue to pray
that she finds her mind
even though daddy done crush the spine
of her personality, in the palms of his hands
but, "a man's got to do, what a man's got to do"
or so went their master plan.
the family man, keeps his family intact
with a pat on the back, or a wack on the ass!
mommy, do you hear me? continue to pray
that she finds her mind
comes back to us one day.
funny, had a son before my period had begun
I was brother's mommy
I was mommy's mum
daddy's having a tantrum
the dishes weren't done
begging us to run
she pays for what we've done.
the shrill of her screams

valery mendes

the violent beat
against the crying wall
the regular police call
of course nothing obscene was seen,
so nothing was done
daddy had won. again.
mommy what's your name?
I pray you don't go insane
don't leave us mommy
can't take this pain that stains my brain
can't think strait
gettin' to school late
wait, my teacher says, I ain't able
to do my timetables
I have no mental capability
rather than emotional disability
I'm academically slow
so
I must join the class, for coloured folk you know
as a mild child...I am passive
but
I'll kick your ass
if anybody called my mama nuts
broken glasses, bloody cuts
is what my so-called playmate gets
for such disrespect.
through blurred eyes
I watched mommy degenerate
a victim of tragic fate
mind rape, love
hate.
then there was the time
his coffee wasn't fine;
so scorching liquid, upon her skin

the price she paid for this deadly sin
burning her externally as well as within...
daddy won. again. mommy what's my name?
Pray that she finds her mind someday
but

I think it would be too late
it seemed years had passed
mommy remained the same
chained, to the frame
of the bed
where she silently read
and the man had done
what the man
had to do
kept his family intact, with the threat of attack
or so we thought
not

he thought he had weeded out her mind
but another grew in time
'cause there's nothing stronger than a mother's love
in silence she planned our escape
she became sane
to ensure her babies weren't slain
in the civil war
for that I adore
and respect my mom
for resisting the self-rival, putting dad on trial
easing the pain that stains my brain
"at least he didn't abandon me", was daddy's plea
of "not guilty"
what a comedy
there is no remedy
for childhood tragedy

can't repay the cost
of innocence lost!
but a decade is gone
the battle is won
mom's a strong, articulate woman
brother's a young man
with the world in his hands
together we laugh at our tragic past
but I must say, daddy, today,
our emotional blood still stains your hands...
my brother wants to be a "family man"
guess that's part of the master plan
what's that my brother?
you love mom, but respect father?
resent her for taking him away?
must be her fault in some way?
women are the weaker sex anyway?
and it's time we let,
"a man do, what a man has to do!"
as women we should shut up and refrain?

I was wrong
what a shame
boys will be boys it seems...
daddy...You've won, again.

Eulogy

Your waxen lips,
They kiss me.
Your ivory fingers,
They touch me.
Your marble eyes,
they look through me.
Tell me, what do they see?

antoinette

Your eyes look right through me,
Deep into my soul,
Tell me,
Can they see,
My life's one and only goal?

To love,
And be loved.
To remember,
And be remembered,
By those who knew my name.

For others to know my life's tale
Carried by the breeze,
The wind,
The gale.
Loving me in their hearts.
Hearing me in their thoughts.
Knowing me in their minds.
Just one person doing this,
Once in a while,
Would bring worth to my daily grinds.

See my tears?
They flow.
Touch my belly,
It trembles.

Will you remember me?
When my days come to an end?
When they put me in the wooden box?
When into the ground I descend?

Will you remember me?
When I have no children to bear my name?
When I have no husband to drive insane?
When my sister forgets my birthday?
When my mother forgets my strange ways?

Say you will,
And if you know you won't,
Lie.
I will remember you
As the days tick by.

But know this:
With your memories,
Your caring,
Your thoughts,
I can never die.

Colour me bad: the experience of a dark skinned woman

I grew up in a family that was unfamiliar with racism. My parents came to the United States from Nigeria in 1972 and moved into "da Bronx". Being first-generation African American made it especially hard to fit in with my peers. Worst of all, my ancestral features became the object of children's laughter.

In America, I've experienced two types of racism: one from White society and the other from my own people. My skin colour has always determined my social status and how people first react to me. I often feel like I'm the last person they want to meet, or that they are doing me some kind of favour by associating with me.

It was a beautiful fall day in early October, and children ran around the school yard during recess. A group of girls were playing double dutch in teams of two, so everyone quickly grabbed a partner. I wasn't the best of players, but I was eager to join in. As I ran to pick a partner, I was stopped by one of the girls, who was huge and bullish. She grabbed my arms and shouted, "You can't play in this game! We don't like the dark-skin girls. They're ugly. You have to be light!" She shoved me out of the playing circle, leaving me alone to watch the game from the steps.

Is this a reality or an insecurity among dark-skinned women? When the subject of skin colour comes up in conversation, I am usually told by those who are light-skinned that I am paranoid. However, among my dark-skinned friends, there is a mutual understanding about the issue. Many have faced

ibiyomi jegede

devastating situations that were beyond their control. I know I'm not bugging out.

In my opinion, Black men are sometimes subconsciously more attracted to light-skinned Black women. During my first year of college, two of three friends that I hung out with were fair-skinned and one was brown-skinned. It wasn't until we took part in social events that I began to recognize differences in people's responses to us. Men were more apt to pay close attention to my light-skinned friends than me and my other friends. At parties, guys would ask my lighter friends to dance, rather than any of us from the "dark posse". This was a continuous cycle.

I was a self-hater. I despised myself because of the color of my skin. I wanted to kill those who were of a lighter complexion, and do you know why? Because people loved the children with the light skin and the long, wavy black hair. "Oh! What a pretty little child, and she got good hair." I was the one people called Dark Vaida or Kizzy from Roots, the one Whoopi Goldberg imitated in her stand-up with a mop on her head, wishing she could be something that she wasn't. I represented the sambos and the mammies of the world! I used to get both Black and White dolls, and I would only play with the White ones, because they were the "prettiest", with long, luxurious hair. And I, too, wanted the "prettiest" of long blond hair and big blue eyes...

Unfortunately, my parents were not aware of the situation that was before them. They were too busy being the wonderful people that they are, working to support their children. Color complexes were uncommon in Nigeria until the early 1980's, when the Eurocentric image reached its height. Nigerian women began to bleach their skin in exchange for the love and attraction of a man. They wanted long, straight hair and a lighter shade of skin to woo their mates. In return, they got blotching skin. ILL!

To this day, these experiences have mentally affected me and my family members. Must we wait for the "in thing" to be dark skin? Or can we as African people learn to love ourselves in every shade?

sweetness

Apple pie
Is as sweet as it can be
But not as sweet as a brother
in a bow tie.

Take out the fries
Eat it with your fingers
Slop it
Let it drizzle down
Ooooh No!
You need a doggy bag.

frances opoku

UN-controllable

Bitch! Ho! Slut!
This is not who I am,
And that is who I'll never be!
I ain't your bitch,
So don't go on like you own me
You better learn to address me respectfully!

Just because you've got your "manhood" to prove
My will or my legs will not move!
You might rape my body,
But you'll never rape my soul.
For that is not who I am
And that's who I'll never be!

There have been others before
And there'll be many more,
So don't try and play me
for your own personal whore.

I ain't waiting for no man
To show me "the way"
Telling me…
    how to dress
    how to walk
    how to act
    what to say?
I alone am the ruler of my own mind and heart.
My spirit and soul will always run free,
And never become what you want them to be!

marta kateri ferede

holding out on stereotypes

melissa smith

"Shooter described as male, Black, about 18, 5'8", wearing dark blue pants..."

"Police seeking two young males of dark complexion. Wearing hooded sweatshirts, one green, the other with large black and white checks..."

"Shooter described as Black, 21-23 years old, 6'0", slim build and short shaved black hair. Wearing yellow baseball cap and yellow satin bomber-type jacket with the word 'Lakers' on the back, yellow baggy jeans and a thick yellow gold chain with large medallion in the shape of a gun..."

I cannot recall how many times I've turned on the radio, tuned into the television or even opened up a newspaper only to hear or see descriptions like these. This seems to be becoming a trend in today's popular culture—one I take offense to: the portrayal of young Black males as ignorant, repulsive, immoral and so on. Don't get me wrong, I'm not trying to say that there aren't some Black males who actually do fall into this category. But when society as a whole is generalizing and saying that they all do, something has to be done.

The question is, "How do we go about changing that?" The few movies that have Black characters and that actually make it to the big screen often leave one with the impression that most

Blacks are drug dealers, pimps, welfare recipients, gangsters, etcetera. Sadly, the small number of Black males that are the cause of this negative stereotyping are bold and indifferent to the damage caused by the crimes they commit, causing embarrassment to the majority, who shudder when they hear the word Black—then "shooter", "robber"," murderer","rapist" in the same sentence.

Up until last month, following the Todd Baylis incident, a day did not go by when the front section of the *Toronto Star* did not contain a picture of a Black man who had been deported back to his homeland. Unfortunately, people like Stephen Martin, a 23-year-old Trinidadian, got the short end of the stick. Stephen came to this country to visit, liked what he saw, and stayed on (in bad judgement) illegally. He's made an outstanding contribution to Canadian society as a youth leader and community volunteer. He has excellent scholastic and athletic records, which more than demonstrate his positive influence on our society. He's accomplished more than most Canadian-born youths, yet he's being sent home without a thought.

What people don't realize is that evil has no set colour, shape, size, or form. It just lurks around, ready to pounce when its next victim comes along. Evil does not discriminate, for there's a black sheep in every family. Which brings me to a point that is not stressed enough: our use of the words 'Black' and 'White'. In a variety of dictionaries the definition of black is: "dark, evil, sombre, dishonourable, deadly." Naturally, white has an opposite meaning. It's defined as: "light, good, fair, pure, innocent, trustworthy." What is wrong with this picture? If you can answer that question you've already taken a step in the right direction—towards change.

Gangsta BITCH, diVa HIP HOP, goddESSES & eARth WOMen & HIP HOP CULTURE

Maxine This is an interview with Motion (Wendy Braithwaite). We're talking about Hip Hop and the Hip Hop culture. Motion, I wanted to skip what Hip Hop is about, because that's an obvious question. I just wanted to get down to the nitty gritty. So let's talk about Snoop Doggy Dog and artists as such, with lyrics like: "There's some freaks in the livingroom getting it on, They're not leaving 'till 6 in the morning. So what 'cha gonna do? You know I got some rubbers in my pocket and my home boys do too." What about lyrics like that? If you've seen the video there's also some young women being led into a bedroom. My question is, as young women—and I'm assuming you're a feminist...

motion Well, I, um, I never...

maxine You've never called yourself a feminist? Okay, as women—and, in my case a feminist and a lesbian, how do we with conscience nod our heads to the funk, and disregard the fact that he's disregarding us and oppressing us, trivializing us and objectifying us?

maxine greaves, with motion

motion   I just need to clarify what I mean by Hip Hop. It's a very broad culture, it's a broad term. When you say Hip Hop you know what you're talking about, but if we talk about women and our concept of Hip Hop or rollin' with Hip Hop, we ourselves have to start defining what our roles are in Hip Hop, defining our idea of it, because I think that will give us more to fight against the negatives. Because whenever people talk about women in Hip Hop, the first thing that they deal with is "Bitch, ho, my freak this…" Snoop—or whatever, is just this one artist. Because he is a platinum-selling artist, he's gonna catch a lot of the attention, right? But I think that in order to effectively discuss those questions we can't define Hip Hop according to stardom. Snoop is like a percent, you-know-what-I-mean? When Hip Hop started there were a lot more female MC's than male MC's, you-know-what-I-mean? They were the ones who were at the forefront in a lot of ways, and started this rhythm of doing the DJing like that. When Hip Hop first came about, women and men, it was like, us. We were at the parties, we were in the jams, we were the ones in the park. We were the ones putting up our hands and bigging people up. We were saying the party rap. It was a very together thing as a cultural group, you-know-what-I-mean? I think if more people knew that, especially male artists, then they'd probably start looking at how their lyrics affect the relationships between young Black men and young Black women today. Because, you find that the music became more aggressive, you-know-what-I-mean? More battlin' and stuff if a female wasn't able to stand up with the same type of lyrics that a brother could say, well then she don't have as many skills. Hip Hop was taking another turn. It started out "Everybody stick up your hands common, stick your hands up in the air," I mean, getting the people into it, but then later it started to be like, "Okay now, affirmation of myself, against yourself. So if I wanna dis' you what am I going to dis' you about? I use your sister," you-know-what-I-mean?

maxine   Well, I think that's important, but I don't want to leave out, you know, the political aspects.

motion   No, not at all, not at all…

maxine   I wanted to ask you also, in relation to what you were saying, how then do you explain even the conscious artists who only rap about the political conflicts between the black community and society, and still forget that it's not just the Black man's job, it also includes Black women. Not only Black women as mothers, but as warriors and soldiers and that sort of thing as well.

motion   Well, I don't think that the precedent has been set properly. The society that we live in is very male-centred, you-know-what-I-mean? Because a lot of people look at the era we're comin' out of, they look at the civil rights and the Black Power movement. That was our last big movement, the Black Power movement, but during that time, look at what was going on. Brothers were saying, "Yeah sistahs, yeah, women are queens but hey, don't challenge the brothers, you-know-what-I-mean? Don't challenge the man." If you look at Black religious power movements, there's still a lot of the emphasis on the man as the leader or the man as the head, and that causes a lot of conflicts because the females aren't given their due respect. And that really has a lot to do with White society's fear of the Black man, and with the patriarchal structure of society. But at the same time, White society's fear of the Black man has created conflict between the Black woman and the Black man. They've tried to make it such a way that we'll become enemies of each other.

maxine   In what way?

motion   Well, for instance, there was a time when the image of the mammy was very integral in the upholding of the White societal power structure. The image of the Black woman is as the head of the family, she's the strong one, she's big, you know? She takes care of the Black family, she takes care of the White family, the Black family and the Black men are lazy. That's how they caused rifts between us, because society's patriarchal structure makes us look like we're backwards.

maxine   Do you think there are truths in the Black woman being the head of the family? I mean, in this time, where Black women are sole…

motion   Supporters…

maxine   of the family, supportive financially, emotionally, raising their sons, raising their daughters. Isn't there truth in that?

motion   No it's not a lie, but that's not the way it should be at all, you-know-what-I'm-saying. As Black women, we have no choice but to take that role, and we've been very strong, I mean, we have upheld our community in so many ways. But a son should learn, how to be a man from both a mother and a father because then you get the balance, you learn how to relate both ways, with women and men. A lot of times these brothers who were raised by their mother, they say, "Well, my mother did it so why can't this girl do it?" You-know-what-I-mean? Or the girls that are raised by single families, they carry on the tradition, because that's all they know. It's just become a never-ending cycle, it has become the norm, but it shouldn't be the norm. You're not supposed to have a family with one parent, because it didn't take one parent to make you, so we need both of their mind sets to make us balanced people. That's why I think a lot of the bad things that are going on in our community are because there's not that family unit that is strong. You-know-what-I-mean?

maxine   Just to get back to my question about conscious rappers, don't you think its frustrating that, although Black women are the heads of the families, and women are battling in this patriarchal society and struggling for power, we're still constantly excluded from their analysis of the Black struggle?

motion   From conscious rappers?

maxine   From conscious rappers.

motion   Could you give me an example?

maxine   Like for instance, KRS-1, or Public Enemy. Not to negate the fact that what they have to say is important, but, to date, I've not heard more than "we have to respect our sistahs because they're the mothers of our children," I feel the only time we're included is when it's a woman rapper, and even then sometimes they're still talking about their men, you-know-what-I-mean? We have a whole concept of struggle as a male issue; we are bombarded with this in music and with movies and so on, and we forget that we're even a part of the struggle. So all we talk about is the fact that our men are being beaten and put in jail, which is a reality. But what is also a reality is that our women are being beaten, and not only are they being beaten, they're being raped, and not only are they being raped, they're also being put in jail. This society has a history of violating Black women. And that needs to be acknowledged as a part of our struggle. And a lot of the black artists or black male artists don't acknowledge that struggle.

motion Well, I think that a person who rhymes has to make a decision. They can decide to give the people what they want, what is going to sell, what's going to get the biggest reaction from the crowd, what they already think. Now, we can't place responsibility on the artists to fulfill positive social roles if they haven't fulfilled this thing within their own minds. They're not gonna talk about what they don't know, or what they refuse to know, you-know-what-I'm-saying? I think it's more than just the artist, because Hip Hop is people, the people who are actually singing the rhyme on a record or whatever. So you get someone like KRS-1, KRS-1 is a man, so he's going to come from a male point of view. But then he has many styles that are biggin' up Black women from his point of view, and he goes beyond boundaries as a brother or as a man because most people think "Why should he even bother to say that? It's not gonna make him no money." Like that song called "Ah, Yeah", right? Where he says:
>Don't call me nigger cause some MC's go for this,
>But call me a god 'cause that's what the Black man is.
>Rolling through the forest, it's the hardest lyrical artist,
>Black woman you are not a bitch, you're a goddess.

So women start going, "I'm not a bitch, I'm a goddess!" See, he's saying that "Black man you're a god, and Black woman you're a goddess." So act accordingly, you-know what-I-mean? It will have a lot of impact because he is a respected artist and people will remember it, and it could affect not only your thinking but also your behaviour, you-know-what-I-mean? Then you have somebody else like Jeru who has this song, it's called "The Bitches." When people first hear that they're like "Jeru man, why would you ever say that?" 'cause he just talks pure consciousness. But the song goes like this, "*I'm not talking 'bout the queens, but the bitches. Not the sistahs, but the bitches. Not the young ladies, but the bitches,*" right? And I remember a lot of people were talking about that, saying that Hip Hop women could actually get with that song. He's the first Hip Hop artist who actually started to make a distinction between what a bitch is supposed to be and what a sistah is supposed to be. There's brothers in the community who are dogs, who don't deserve our respect, because of the way that they handle themselves, the way they treat women, the way they see themselves—just as dick machines right? And at the same time we have to admit that there are also a lot of young Black women out there who have no respect for themselves. I was by the pool at a party at "Jack the Rapper" in Atlanta, and I was like, what up with this? 'cause there were sistahs in the pool, takin' off their tops with a whole bunch of brothers standing around, you-know-what-I'm-saying? There are women who are 'hoing' themselves and who are not looking at themselves as sistahs, goddesses or strong Black women—but who are looking at themselves and saying I got two breasts and I got an ass. "This is what I'm going to use to sell myself." And then the brothers are standing around the pool, "Whaaa!" You-know-what-I-mean? (mock laughter) And the girls laughing, with their weaves and stuff. It made me feel embarrassed, but it also let me see that there are a lot of generalizations, that I'm going to have to start to narrow down. We're really going to have to look to see who's ready for this movement, because not everybody is going to be down for it, you-know-what-I-mean? A lot of people are not trying to improve themselves. And sistahs like that give these brothers something to get on the mike and chat about so that other brothers are like "Yeah! Yeah! I know a girl like that!"

maxine But don't you think there's a lack of analysis going on? Look at our community. How many women are survivors of not only incest, but of rape. I'm saying 90% of the women I know have been survivors of rape. And so these are the same women that, because of their histories, have this low self-esteem—"I am not worth anything more than my tits and my ass." There are a lot of sistahs who believe that if they don't whore themselves to all these men, then they are worth absolutely nothing, and so they might as well be dead.

motion   Okay, that's true, but does that justify it? We could flip it and say, well brothers in L.A. could say "White society, they put us into poor communities, they segregated us, put guns in our community, and so we have nothing else to do but shoot each other."

maxine   I'm not trying to negate the Black struggle in terms of men. I'm just trying to look at it in terms of women.

motion   But the reason I was saying that, I was giving an analogy of the cause and effect idea.

maxine   We have to look deeper than, "she was in the pool taking off her clothes." We also have to look at or talk about her history. Is her history the result of her behaviour, or is her behavior the result of her history? You know? We have to look at it that way before we can do any healing to the community. Because if we have sistahs that have been violated to the point where they themselves believe that that's all they are worth, then we're going to have sistahs that take their clothes off. And then when our men call them bitches and ho's…

motion   They think that's their name.

maxine   They take that on, and not only do they internalize it, but they believe that. And they live that. You know? And I feel that it just adds to their violation. You-know-what-I-mean?

motion   Well, I guess what I'm saying at the same time is that I know this is a male-dominated society. I think that's something that we all know. But we have to fully see the circle right? I went to a Hip Hop show, one time, and these two strippers went on stage. I was freaked. These two girls came up there and they stripped on stage, in a Hip Hop jam. I never seen nothin' like that, at least not until then. At the same time the brother, who brought them up, he's a fool obviously. I don't know what type of point he was trying to prove. Then you have the other guys in the isles who are freakin', "Oh my

God! Waaaaaa!" And then you have the two girls on the stage who were totally relishing in it. They weren't thinking, you-know-what-I'm-saying? So what I'm saying is, it comes from a cause, but the effect has got to work itself out. Because let's say there's a guy in the aisles who's never seen anything like that. He knows he never raped any female. His father never raped his sister, or whatever, but he sees two girls up on stage doing that, and he starts thinking "Oh, okay, so they weren't joking in that song I heard the other day." He's not thinking, "Oh, ah, I wonder what happened to her when she was younger." You know?

maxine Yeah, but I'm saying that as a community it is our responsibility. I'm not saying that's the boy's responsibility, and I'm also saying as Black women, it's our responsibility. The cause needs to be acknowledged and dealt with before the effect does.

motion Yeah right. I think it would be my responsibility to talk to a girl and say, "You know what? You know what you were doing up there? This is what was happening." And then the female could say—"Yeah, but I'm getting paid, fuck off." What I'm saying is we've got to start taking responsibility, because nobody is going to save us but us, you-know-what-I'm-saying? Nobody else is going to put their hand out and say "Oh, let me see if I can help you rise up, Black woman." It's only Black women who are going to do that. And if you have sistahs within who are bringing down your strength, those are the sistahs that you need to change, and they gotta go.

maxine That's the thing, we can't get rid of them because we need all the sistahs. And that's why I feel it's really important that we start as women to talk about that. But I think it's also the responsibility of the men to look at that. We've been talking about men a whole lot in this interview, and it's hard to just talk about women.

motion How can we just talk about women? It's like a coin saying "Yo, I'm going to do it with the head but not with the tail." You know, it's like that yin-yang sign. That's two equal parts. Sun and Moon. Day and Night. It's so hard to separate the two of them. If we don't have both those parts, things can't survive.

maxine   I understand that, but what I'm saying is that there is work that needs to be done, strictly and specifically on our Black women in society. We are at the point where we don't even have a sense of self, so that we can sit down and talk about and analyze issues that only relate to us.

motion   When you're talking about issues that only relate to us, what are they?

maxine   Issues like rape.

motion   How can that relate to us…

maxine   That relates to us. That's a violation.

motion   Oh no, no, no—That's a violation of us, yes, but when we talk about rape we're not raping ourselves, it's men who are raping us.

maxine   No, we are not raping ourselves. But we are the survivors of rape and incest, and we have to look at all of that, we have to look at a lot of issues that affect us as women. Look at the different parts of us. Because if you are a Black lesbian, you are totally invisible. There is no such thing as a Black lesbian. You-know-what-I-mean? We also have to look at the power difference in our society. We have little privilege. It's not the same privilege as a man. Those issues contribute to our place in society, our place in the Black community, and that also contributes to the way we relate to our Black men.

motion   Okay that's true, but let's say we talk about rape. Women are the victims of rape. But the thing is, you can't talk about the victim and not the perpetrator of the crime. I don't think it's isolated, because what affects us is going to affect them, and what affects them is going to affect us. What is it that makes a rapist do what he does? Where is he learning those things from? Is he learning it from a father, from T.V.? Is he learning it from watching women in peep shows?

maxine   What I'm saying is, why don't we have that in-depth analysis of why women do what women do? Like standing by the pool naked. We don't say, "Okay, so what was her history? Why does she do that?" We would go into that for men, always. And that's what I mean—getting back to the rap artists—a large percentage of people listen and internalize and take on what they're putting out.

motion   Well they have to be challenged, and in general people have to be educated. Because people write movies, write books, rap lyrics, whatever according to what their education and experience is, or what they're motivated by. Now if what makes you motivated is to drink your 40's and talk about ho's, and ho's you never even had, that's what you write about. Sex and stuff like that sell, so that's what you're going to give them. If you're an educated person, if you're a conscious person, if you're a spiritual person you want to write about the things that you're dealing with, like Black power, or Black business. Or it could be things that are a lot more subtle, talking about killing the things in society that are oppressing us. What I'm seeing is more lyricists who have stuff to say. That's why you get somebody like KRS-1, because he uses his lyrics to educate. So its not just entertainment, because it's like he sees the power of art. It's like in the 60's—you know how people used to call each other "man"? "Yo, what's up man?" That was something important, because before we were being called "boy". Then in the 90's, women started calling themselves "earths", you-know-what-I-mean? It's like, you're not a girl, you're the earth. You're nature. That came out through Hip Hop. A lot of negative things come out, but you also see certain positive movements going on.

maxine   But not just through male artists, but also artists like MC Lyte, whom I adore. And Queen Latifah.

motion   When she came out with "U.N.I.T.Y.", that was like an anthem. That was when we were coming out of the gansta rap era. And gansta rap was, well, quote unquote "gangsta rap" and so certain shit was comin' up, and she came on "Who you callin' a bitch?" in "U.N.I.T.Y.". She was talking about unity between Black women and Black men, educating them and challenging them. In that song she doesn't just point to the men as the perpetrators of the bitch/ho mentality, she gives three different scenarios: Violence against women by brothers ("Why wear yourself out brother, beating her up?") and then another one about how brothers talk to you on the street, how they just assume, "Yo, come here bitch." The last one is about females taking on this new image of the gangsta bitch: "Yo, I'm gonna turn this around, Yeah, I'm a bitch, so what?" But the thing is that there's not enough females out there who are comin' out. Every now and then you get a trickle of females, but in this industry it's always been like, there would be one good female, or two, but there can be no more than three. They say "female MC", but they don't say "male MC's", you-know-what-I-mean? When you put female and male before it, it's like showing which one is the norm. A female MC is the novelty or the exception. Now you finally get Nefertiti, and just the name alone, well, you don't have to know what she's saying.

maxine   What about Brat?

motion   She's comin' out. She's going for hers and she's sounding like that Snoop. She has his flow and everything, but it's too bad, because if she came out first people would be on her bra strap. Like, "Yaaaaa! She's bad", but because he came out first, he's supposed to be the norm. But then I've heard her songs and she's not really down with anything.

maxine   Exactly.

motion   But the fact is I don't see her dealing with the negative things either. I mean, figure it out.

maxine   But she does call herself Bitch and she calls herself Ho and Pimp.

motion   Oh, no, I didn't know that.

maxine   Yeah, and she does have a song, you know "Funk-de-Fie"? Where she says she's: "the baddest little pimp in the Hip Hop biz." To me that's just like she's internalizing.

motion   And basically she's using what she thinks is the norm, 'cause she wants to be respected.

maxine   By men.

motion   Yeah, right, because they're the ones who are looked at as the consumers even though it's really females who buy Hip Hop. The brothers tape it off each other. They couldn't be bothered to put their money down and buy the tapes, you-know-what-I-mean? I really haven't listened to enough of her lyrics. But if that's what she's dealing with, she's just trying to do what she thinks will sell. 'Cause I know as an artist it's difficult because you want people to respect you, you want people to say, "yeah that girl has skills", but a lot of times in order to do that, you feel that you have to say what everybody else is saying. What you know is going to get the reaction. They don't want to be preached to, they don't want to hear, "I'm a Black female and you better respect me." You have to be very strong to be a female in this business. Make your voice be heard, you-know-what-I-mean?

Why sistahs don't like to NIKE

"How do I love de blk man...let me count the de ways...daze, phaze I'm in, maze I sin...let me flow from my end to our begin..."

SCOPIN':   Wut 2 do? Wut 2 do 'bout dat man?
ebony prince/sable bliss/
milk chocolate treat/ so sinfully sweet/
good enuff 2 eat in a single bite/
i'm damned if i do/and damn i just might/
succumb 2 your blkness/your sheer stark delight/
not even touchin'/steal a quick glance/
don't fight me/blk man/pleeze/like a dream
i feel naked/like a woman/
i feel true love/you're my meridian
my scared abyss the light consumin' my
hauntin, darkness
you're my meridian
my african king from which my spirit
enchantedly springs
a rhythmic pulse enters your being and
penetrates my soul/don't let go/go slow/
i feel naked/woman /smouldering heat/as we
dance we stroke/as we stroke we make love/
kiss me/kiss me/kiss me/like you shouldah

sistah caroline

should
shower me like a nubian queen
treasure my virginity
Isis's box of my womanhood

DICK CRAVIN': Lurkin' in the thick blk mist of the savannah grasslands i became moist while i watched wide-eyed as you became increasin'ly hard. Like the forbidden passion fruits of cush you tempted i for i heaved to let you in. The pain and the pleasure of i is the virgin's sin. Talk dirty to me baby. Talk dirty to me. dirty. talk. The more afraid i become the more alluring you wouldah cum.
TITS
ASS
TONGUE
I want it soooo sweet that i itch sooooo deep you must scratch me beneath the skin. Stroke my thigh darlin'. Stroke my thigh. stroke. thigh.
BADD
REAL BADD
Lick me down 'til i flow like the niger and nile as one. Take me tonight. Take me. Take. Slow. Blk. Hard. Long. Sting the snake into my apple 4 ever strong!

FUNK DAT BUDDIE: acceleration. stop. acceleration. don't stop. blk magic/ kneading/
cinnamon breast feeding/
steamy red roses,
salty ice-cream,
deep mystic dungeons where a chocolate
covered tongue plunges into orifices

                    unknown to womankind.
                        acceleration. stop. acceleration.
                            don't stop. guide me/too
                            dreamy zones
                            in twilight over and
                            above silky smooth naked:
                            THIGHS
                            LEGS
                            TUMMIES
                            REARS
                    and the sacred sword of shaka ZULU!
                    Oyster. chew. chew.
                    i in a blk tux with tails/you in
                    blk lace and heels...wut a man!
                    acceleration. stop. acceleration.
                    don't stop. harder we fight/harder
                    we cum!/take me to de end of de universe
                    to de muthaland and back/
                    dive into my centre soooo hard that
                    i turn inside out and land with my
                    butt in the air and your 15 inch tongue
                    in my mouth
eyes
    lips
        eyes
            footsies between our
cheeks/body/buddie/panther/blk man/firm&ripe/hard/
explosion/taut/ stacked/grinding/hot sex on a platter/
wut does it matter if i never breathe again/

REVERSAL OF A DOG: poison a female pimp a gurly studd when you's got a hard prick who needs love/you thought your boyz were down wit opp you haven't seen opp 'til you's been wit me/and when i say "been" there ain't no turnin' back/until dis dogg reaches climax/i'm brutal savage ruff/befo' i get started you'll be screamin' nuff!/i'm goin' to work you dogg like the funkin' marines/i'll have you on all fours barkin' like benji!/i cum hardcore and when a man makes love to me he becomes the:

WHORE
BITCH
HOOCHIE ASS SKEEZER SLUT
i like to be licked/kissed/and gently stroked/befo'
i start cookin' and producin' smoke/i'm on top/
your below/now you know exactly whose in control/
i'll tell you i love you/of course it's a line/to
git your big blk dick between my succulent thighs/
work it brotha/shake that ass/i'll ram you hard/i'll
slam you fast/brown suga' here's a word to the wise/
love makin' is about me gettin' satisfied/once my
G spot is hit/it's on to the next MALE HO/the next
MALE BITCH/female ruff neck/gangstah hoodie/scopin'
da place for some fresh blk booty/rapin' men if dey
won't give it up/and if you say no i'll still tell
my gurls we bucked/why you sweatin' G feelin' violated
degrated created to breed/welcome to a sistah's world/
my daily routine/bein' dogged by some brotha's that
only see P-U-S-S-Y/welcome to a blk woman's world/
now brotha... I mean NIGGAH/be a man and ask yourself
why!/

"HOW DO WE LOVE BLK MAN? EACH SISTAH HAS HER OWN PLAN. LOVE AND SEX WUT A MESS I MUST CONFESS AS AN EX-HOTTIE TENDER RONI FULL OF BOLONI GANGSTAH BITCH WITH A SWITCH THAT TALKED WITH STREET SLANG 'CAUSE LIKE LL SAID I'M FROM AROUND THE WAY. I LOVED TO KNOCK BOOTS SHOOT HOOPS AND SHOOP SHOOP ALL NITE LONG SUPER FREAK WAS MY FAVOURITE SONG 'CAUSE I WAS A NASTY GURL IN MY OWN LITTLE NASTY WORLD WHO SPOKE ABOUT LADIES FIRST BUT HAD TO HAVE BACK PRETTY BROWN EYES AND THE DUCETS IN MY PURSE. CAN'T GET PRINCE TO GET OFF TO PUT ON THE BODY BAG SAYS ITS A DRAG A STYLE TO CRAMP. THAT'S WHY SALT N' PEPA SAID MOST MEN ARE TRAMPS. YOU WANT TO TAKE A SEXUAL TRIP WITH A HONEY DIP 'CAUSE WE SO HORNEY BUT BLK BABIES ARE HAVIN' BABIES AND IT'S THE

SAME OLD STORY. THE DAYS OF SEXUAL HEALING ARE FASTLY DEPLETING THAT'S WHY I CAN'T NIKE! IT'S AGAINST MY SISTAH PSYCHE! X-RAY LOOKS LITTLE BLK BOOKS…JOOK AND JOOK AND JOOK…I'LL BREATHE AGAIN…IF WE FUCK AGAIN AND IF WE FUCK AGAIN…WE MAY END."

HERE SHE COMES

sherrie owtten

Who is that woman
who thinks she's
Alll that?
When she walks by
men turn their heads
both White and Black.
She walks with her head held high
to look better than us.
She walks with a switch
filling men's heads with lust.
Who is that woman
who thinks she's **Alll** that?
She has a beautiful figure
and her pockets are fat.
Everyone's asking who she could be
look out girl friends, boyfriends
that woman is me!
I'll tell you right now
you have mixed up your facts.
I don't walk down the streets
thinkin' I'm **Alll** that.
I walk with my head held high because
I'm proud of who I am—

Thank you very much.
When I walk with that switch,
it does not make me any man's breakfast, dinner dessert or lunch!
I have a beautiful figure
and my pockets are fat,
but that does not mean I think I'm **Alll** that!
You only whisper and talk because you know
I'm bad and correct.
I am not a tramp or a ho.
I am the essence of woman.
I demand both power and respect!

● ●

I AM

tonia bryan / nicole redmian

i am honey, cinnamon
and fresh ginger

I am sweet sorrel
and fragrant rose
I am rough mauby bark
and smooth ebony
Black as night

I am **brash, loud, rude**
and **hot to the touch**

I am the lips you tasted
for the very first time
soft, sweet and girlish
like your own

I am a grade school sistah
invitin' you over

to show you the size
of my thirteen year old muscles

I am **your best girlfriend and you**
down behind your parent's place
kissin' and makin' out

I am a college room-mate sleepin'
in your bed one night
wearing nothin'
but my naked skin
askin' you to
"Please rub my back, sweet heart?"

I am long walks in the woods
we hold hands and you lay me down
touchin' here, lickin' there
ahhhhhhh

I am not **your mother** tellin' you
'bout some woman's
wedding in white

askin' for the **millionth time**
"when are you plannin'
on tyin' the knot?"

demandin' for the **billionth time**
that you present her with a grandchild
before she meets her maker
NOT NOW MA
I HAVE A HEADACHE
I am MYSELF
stranger and friend
closest confidant, bitterest enemy

I am MYSELF
WIRY, resistant, resilient and arrogant

Do you know me?
Can you deal with me?
With what I am?
With who you are?

I am **MORE** than a mere ten percent
of the country's population

more than a best friend or a college chum

I am honey, cinnamon
and fresh ginger
on your tongue

I am sweet sorrel and fragrant rose
filling your senses

I am rough mauby bark as we rub
sweaty and urgent
skin to skin

I am BLACK ebony coming to your arms
with the fullness of the moon
in the darkness of the night

I am a **Wicca warrior**
a **Zami queen**

I am screaming like a
B.A.N.S.H.I.I.

I AM EVERY WOMAN.

SUBliminal demise

Many faces
isolation
isolated by fragile infantile fantasy;
many sleep with eyes open
copin' with the pain that stains the brain
don't recognize my voice, can't see my face
rapid life pace, feel the blood race
treading water
a tragic existence
physical resistance.
fight with spiritual persistence;
emotional prey, emotional play
condone alone, the altitude of solitude
elevation, revelation
of the insane truth: afraid to die, yet afraid to live
confess the ironic light of knowledge
of self
don't recognize my voice, can't see my face
a case
of dysfunctional illusion, fusion
of silence and noise
confusion
sweet and sour delusion
laws of survival
resist the self
rival, self-righteous primal desire, to see, to flee
to bind, to find
the blind scent of identity, reality. reality?

valery mendes

two dimensional sensuality
to touch you, is not to know you
don't recognize my voice, can't see my face;
the path's been set for me
destructive destiny
self-fulfilling prophecy = tragedy.
another ocean swallows her island
treading water, a tragic existence
fight with spiritual persistence; drowning pride,
stifling time, shallow lies
subliminal demise
don't swallow me
part the sea
of destiny.
'cause I don't recognise my voice, can't see my face;
I wait, with no destination
lonely anticipation
a desperate situation
craving the noise that silences silence
unaware of welcome, agitated, frustrated by still
driven by will
to uprise, and surprise, and survive.
but I don't recognize my voice, can't see my face
disgrace.
hear the echoing shrill of quiet
passive riot
the crashing thrash of calm
pin drops, and i, shake the pain: fear, blame, shame.
still I don't recognize my voice, can't see my face;
a case of mental intrusion, physical exclusion
unaccessible solution
seeking spiritual evolution
above the clenches of tyrannic reality, and preordained mediocrity...
my video eyes
embraced by lies
are coated in self-despise...
I wonder, I ponder, imagine...I wonder, not when...I wonder, not
when...I wonder, not when
but "if"
I shall rise, from my subliminal demise!

daRLiNg

Darling flying on the dragon,
Darling sitting down,
Darling singing lovely song—
Darling's underground.

Darling laying in wooden box,
Darling with arms crossed,
Darling always stays so still
Darling's underground.

Darling blinks,
Darling sighs,
Yet beneath the hardened ground she lies
Darling's underground.

Darling feels much hunger,
Darling starts to cry,
Darling's lost her dolly.
Darling's lost her mind.

antoinette

to christine

i wish I could tell you
That you're not too fat
That you're fine the way that you are
That you're pretty enough
And you don't have to wear punishing heels
I wish I could make you believe
That you don't have to starve yourself
Or add to your chest
To fit this year's fashions.
And I wish I could tell you,
To love yourself as much as you love him.
You don't have to make yourself
Into his ideal
The real you is worth so much more.
But I am only one voice,
Against so many
The magazines with diets and makeovers
That you read
The fairy tale your mother read you,
Where the mermaid gave her voice
To be what the prince wanted.
Oh, I wish I could make you listen
But I'm only one voice
Drowned out by so many.

susan forde

Sister-Sister

joi-elle diunnah

Have you ever gone to a party, sat in a train, walked into a store and met the piercing eyes of a sister? She glares at you in silence as if you owed her something, stole her man, or were wearing her best frock. We have all been on the giving and receiving end of that ill-toed line. Are you conscious of the bridges you are building and do you want to continue to stain the mirrored image of yourself?

I am outraged at the harsher realities that make it increasingly difficult for me to fight and find Sister-Sister. I have no regrets about pursuing this woman thing. It is something we should all be aware of. Something we all need to share.

Lately, I have been wondering why it is so hard for Black women to form a united front and to love one another. I observe my mother and father, my sisters and brothers, and I am awed at the irreversible bond that we share. I have loved them and the love they made me feel, but longed for the day that I would find a true Sister-Sister.

I wanted to laugh with her. I wanted to vent to her about the sorry boy I loved. I wanted to share with her my experiences with frizzy hair, nappy roots, ashy legs, hot combs and hair grease. Sometimes I ached inside, other times I cried out loud. I was brave enough to be a friend and I deserved to have one. I remember the pain with joy and contempt.

Where are you Sister-Sister? She stands on the platform with a sweet/sour attitude and her feelings clashing. She is critical of my clothes, my education, my religion, my job and my God-given beauty. She is quick to pass judgement, which is most often negative. She truly wants to exemplify a genuine friend, but has lost concern with uplifting my spirits. She is content as long as we are toe-to-toe on the same level, but becomes disenchanted when I take a step in a different direction. A new job, a boyfriend, a marriage, a baby and even a house are all grounds for desertion. The better choice, of course, would be for her to use my success to boost herself, and vice versa, but somehow we always forget, finding it easier to grab for the attention allotted to another.

I believe an overwhelming majority of us are guilty of using this tactic to suffocate Sister-Sister. It is the glue that keeps our head above water and our self-esteem intact. We have planted seeds and given root to the rise of the silent revolution as we move from minutes to hours, slide from days to months, and jump from years to decades, snubbing one another ever so silently.

I think it's time we joined the tour and stopped hovering on the brink of restlessness. I know that we are conscious of ourselves and are exploring our differences.

Mixed messages do nothing to heighten our awareness or change our points of view. So it is absolutely necessary that we recognize each other's commitments and strife. Seize the moment to smile and celebrate Sister-Sister with a heartfelt array of unconditional love. Discover that a lifelong friendship among kindred spirits is invaluable.

I encourage you to come full circle and tap into the value taught to us as children. You may find that we can find safety in each other's arms and minds, while illuminating our self-esteem in the highest form of unity.

For now, I myself have vowed to hang onto my schoolgirl reflections of my sister's success and draw strength from them. I will do this without trying to drain her. It is not my intention to give birth to a power struggle. We, womankind, are not about that. I will mirror her and she hopefully will mirror me. And perhaps, we will finally meet Sister-Sister by the open door. One of us will arrive ahead of the other, but always with the same goal in mind. Voices together, strong and kind!

Bios...

Titilola Adebanjo (Titilola means "forever my wealth") is a fifteen-year-old with two supportive parents.

Suzanne Anderson is a Black Woman/Sister writing poems and prose. A Woman-loving Sister, who makes sense of the world through her writing.

Antoinette is a unique and proud mixture of Native Indian, Caribbean Black and French Canadian. She says, "My upbeat and charismatic approach to life, as well as my extremely supportive friends and family, have kept me going in my quest to become a writer and to build the world's first life-size house of Lego."

Rose-Ann Bailey is twenty-three years old, Jamaican by birth, she has lived in Canada for the past nineteen years. She is currently enrolled in university in the Fine Arts Department majoring in Photography.

Camille Bailey is a twenty-year-old poet, Sistah-Lover and student of life.

Anna Bauer I was born in Toronto, Canada, on July 31, 1971. I spent ten of my early years in Kingston, Jamaica, the land of my mother's family. I returned to Canada to attend high school. I have recently opened a clothing store on Queen Street. I am currently a contributing writer to two Toronto magazines, *Venue* and *FIN Magazine*.

Tonya Bryan and Nicole Redman are two Lesbian Sistahs who co-founded *Da Juice*, a magazine for Black Dykes.

Ngardy Conteh was born in 1978 in Freetown Sierre Leone, West Africa. She moved to Toronto, Canada at the age of three. She is now attending Vaughan Road Collegiate Institute. Ngardy is an aspiring track and field athlete and hopes to someday have a career in journalism.

Nicole Curling is presently studying Multi-media at the Vancouver Film School.

Tara Darrall I was born in Canada and lived twenty of my twenty-three years there. The other three years I spent in Jamaica. In May of 1995, I graduated from McMaster University with an honours degree in Sociology. My aim is to continuously search out those things that I truly have a passion for.

Wendy Davis is a student and aspiring writer.

Joi-Elle Dinnall has been writing for a long time. She studied Journalism in College. Her work has been published in a variety of magazines and newspapers.

Jillian M. Dixon is nineteen years old, moved to Vancouver six months ago from "a lot of places," and is happy her family has taken her back in.

Tovah Leiha Dixon is a fifteen-year-old from Halifax. A Virgo, she lives with her mother, two brothers and three sisters.

Siobhan Douglas is a fifteen-year-old, grade ten student at Oakwood Collegiate High School in Toronto. She enjoys reading and writing and is planning on pursuing a career in Criminology.

Natalie Eta is seventeen and was born in Toronto, Canada. She is in her last year of high school in a City alternative school. She plans to attend the University of Toronto. **First Ride** is her first published work.

Susan Forde I am eighteen years old. I was born in Guyana and immigrated to Canada when I was nine years old. I lived with my father and stepmother. She died when I was fifteen, and I moved out on my own, living on student welfare and attending high school. In the fall, I will be attending the University of Toronto to study Psychology and French.

Marta Kateri Ferede I was born in Addis Ababa, Ethiopia, October 1974, to Desta (which means "happiness" in Amharic), and Getachew Ferede. We moved to Canada when I was seven years old in the dead of winter. You can imagine what a shock that was to my little African soul.

Paula Avril French was born in Leeds, England. She moved to Toronto twenty years ago at the age of six. She continues to write stories.

Natasha Gomez-Bonner has been writing poetry for the past two years. This is her first published piece.

Maxine Greaves is a twenty-two year-old Black Lesbian living and loving in Toronto. She has a five-year-old daughter.

Carol Higgins I was born in Toronto. I am twenty-three years old. For the past two years I have been involved in a joint programme with York University and Seneca College in Communication Arts. I am looking forward to graduating from both institutions.

Jennifer S. Holland was born in Montreal in 1976. She is nineteen years old and completing the Community Worker Programme at George Brown College of Applied Arts and Technology.

Lisa Hollingsworth I am currently a student at the University of Toronto, where I plan to obtain a Bachelor of Science degree. For the past five years I have been a dancer with the Afro-Caribbean Dance Ensemble. I composed my poems while attending St. Mary Catholic Secondary School. I have always been inspired by Maya Angelou.

IJose I am a poet and visual artist born in Nigeria. I've been living in Toronto for the past two years. Born to a Nigerian mother and a Chinese father, I started writing from the young age of eight, probably from the aloneness I felt as a result of my parental and social isolation. I am also a pioneer mentor of MatRika, a women poet's group.

Ibiyomi Jegede was born in Nigeria. She currently lives in the United States.

Erica Lawson I was born in Jamaica, on January 7th, 1967. I came to Canada in 1981, completed high school and went on to Carleton University. I graduated in 1990 with a B.A. in Political Science and Sociology. I am currently employed as a counsellor. I have a lifelong affair with books—my passion is reading. I enjoy writing and would like to develop my skills in this area. My dream is to write enough short stories to publish my collection—someday. My big, big dream is to live in a house by the Atlantic Ocean, somewhere in Africa where I can spend my time reading and writing (sigh).

Karen Lee   Born in Jamaica in 1971, she is now actively involved in the performing arts, including poetry and dance and is a singer in the Griot Chorale in Toronto. With her Honours B.A. in History and African Studies from York University, she remains committed to issues of African women, youth and culture in her work and volunteer experience. She is an aspiring lecturer and writer.

Charmaine Lewis   is a Black lesbian born and bred in Trinidad and Tobago. A poet, a designer and a creative soul, she believes no stone shall be left unturned. A Capricorn, she can only see herself climbing to the top of the mountain. She is free. She is wild. She is out, and she is celebrating the steadiness of her balance. She says: "My appreciation goes out to Sister Vision Presss for their commitment and love to the Women's community."

Makeda Lewis   is a fifteen-year-old student. She enjoys school and is planning to pursue a career in Social Work.

Mansa   I have been writing most of my life. I am a Creative Writing student at York University.

Lorraine Anne McLeod   I am twenty-four years old and I was born and raised in Toronto. Both of my parents are Jamaican. I recently graduated from York University with a B.A. in English. I currently work as a youth worker, but would eventually like to become an English teacher. I have been writing poetry for almost twelve years and hope some day to have a book of poetry published.

Valery Mendes   I was born in Canada but never felt Canadian. I am a visual artist, writer and poetess. I am twenty-three, a single parent and a university student. Much of my work is a direct expression of my feelings and views, which I trace back to my problematic childhood and current life issues affecting me as a non-white female. My works often comment on issues of power and oppression, namely domestic violence, discrimination, and self-abuse.

Ellaree Metz lives in Toronto.

Nicole Minerve   As the dark mahogany of her skin and the clay redness of her lips show her heritage: African—so does the writing of her poetry reflect her gift for looking into people's souls to find the majestic silence.

Motion   is a sister with a vision who daily re-evaluates concepts of truth, knowledge and wisdom. Involved with poetry, music, media, and community organizations, Motion has realized the beauty and power of Black traditions, especially those which manifest today in the language, art, music, movement and message of the Hip Hop generation. As co-founder of Black List Music, an independent, artist-run label, Motion has performed for the past seven years with The Nu Black Nation.

Asha Noel   I was born in Trinidad, March 1977, but I have spent most of my life in Canada. Here, I have participated in many activities: dance, music, soccer, conferences on racism, sexism, multiculturalism and the unity of Canada. I graduated from Fredericton High School, New Brunswick, with an Academic Black F, (honour roll). I will be attending the University of Toronto, where I received an entrance scholarship. I am enrolled in the International Development Co-op Programme and plan on doing my year of work experience somewhere in the Caribbean.

Frances Opuku   I attend Cardinal Newman High School. I am sixteen years of age. In my spare time I like to draw and write poems. My favourite poet is Maya Angelou. Writing poems is one of my favourite hobbies. After high school I would like to pursue a profession in lab technology.

Kim Outten   I am a young Black writer of eighteen years. I've been writing seriously since I was ten years old. Since then I have continued to write from my heart and imagination. I am truly grateful for the opportunity that Sister Vision Press has given me.

Sherrie Outten   is eighteen years old. She uses writing as a medium to express opinions and experiences. She says, "As a young Black Woman I am honoured to have my voice heard through **Black Girl Talk**."

Jay Pitter is a twenty-four year-old author, poet and playwright. Her first book was independently published in February of 1991. She has hosted poetry readings at elementary schools, high schools, and post secondary institutions. Jay has performed at the First International Dub Poetry Festival, Poetry and Jazz nights, and at the Toronto Arts Council. She has donated her time to projects such as Our Black Story and tutoring for community organizations. It is her sincere desire to use her artistic talents as a vehicle to promote healthy attitudes in the community at large.

Marie-Jolie Rgwigema Didas Gemeni is twelve years old. She is an Ethiopian-born Rwandan. She lives with her mother, who is separated, and an older brother.

Shelley Rodney I am a high school student who enjoys writing. I am happy to be a part of this anthology.

Ayoola Silvera is twenty years old. She reads anything and everything anywhere anytime. She works in her most favourite place, five different libraries in the city. She wants to write, read and live happily ever after.

Keisha Silvera I am a young Black woman struggling to complete high school and to get on with the things I love to do: theatre, writing, photography, travelling, and talking with people.

Sistah Caroline i am wombmon/womb/blk/i am klan/of stolen afrikkans/on stolen land/my revolution is poetry/plays/community activism/red&blk power/theatrical performance/i hold a B.A.A. in radio and television arts/i am currently working on my B.Ed. in Fine Arts/i want to fulfill my journey as a healer/teacher/artist/warrior woman/for red&blk youth.

Melissa E. Smith I am a full time high school student. I was born March 23rd, 1979 in Montreal, Quebec. I speak English, French and Italian, in the hopes that I will be able to become an interpreter in the United Nations. I have five siblings. This is the first of my work to be published.

Stacey Tingle is Canadian born. She is a student at Humber College studying Multi-media. Aware of the struggles of Sistahs living in North America and the World, she keeps alive through poetry.

Roxanne Tracy I am a twenty-one year-old fourth-year student at York University, majoring in both Mass Communication and Anthropology. I see a future career for myself in the legal aspects of human rights. This is the first time that I have had my work accepted for book publication, and I am determined to keep writing.

Yvette Trancoso I am twenty-four years old and was born in Toronto to Trinidadian parents. I am a graduate of York University. Currently I am editor-in-chief of In Other Words...Literary Quarterly.

Wendy A. Vincent I received my B.A. from York University in 1994. I was born in Ontario, on November 4, 1970 (Scorpio!!!).

Monique Wilson teaches piano. She has won two international poetry contests. She says, "I just write and others see the importance of my words, sometimes even before I do." She hopes to study English in University.

All efforts have been made to trace the copyright holders for the following: (We would appreciate any information that would enable us to do so) Joi-Elle Dinnall — Sporting Womanhood and Sister-Sister; Ijose — The Pussy is Ours; Suzanne Anderson — Memory-Bank Movies and Going Without; Ellaree Metz — Rainbow of Love and Hit of Poison; Tonia Bryan and Nicole Redman — I Am; Wendy Davis — Uncontrollable Feeling.